THE PALACE OF DREAMS

THE PALACE OF DREAMS

ISMAIL KADARE

TRANSLATED FROM
THE FRENCH OF JUSUF VRIONI
BY BARBARA BRAY

ARCADE PUBLISHING • NEW YORK

FIRST ARCADE PAPERBACK EDITION 1998

First published in Albania in 1981 under the title *Nepunesi i pallatit te endrrave*

Library of Congress Cataloging-in-Publication Data

Kadare, Ismail
    [Nepunesi i pallatit te endrrave. English]
    The palace of dreams / Ismail Kadare; a novel written in Albanian and translated from the French of Jusuf Vrioni by Barbara Bray.
       p.   cm.
    Originally published: New York : William Morrow and Co., 1993.
    ISBN 1-55970-416-0
    1. Totalitarianism—Fiction. 2. Balkan Peninsula—Fiction. I. Bray, Barbara. II. Title.
PG9621.K3N4413   1998
891'.9913—dc21   97-29724

Published in the United States by Arcade Publishing, Inc., New York
Distributed by Little, Brown and Company

10 9 8 7 6 5 4 3 2 1

BP

PRINTED IN THE UNITED STATES OF AMERICA

CONTENTS

THE PALACE OF DREAMS

M O R N I N G

. . .

The curtains were letting in the uncertain light of dawn, and as usual he pulled up the blanket in the hope of dozing on a while longer. But he soon realized he wouldn't be able to. He'd remembered that this sunrise heralded no ordinary day, and the thought drove away all desire for sleep.

A moment later, as he groped by the bed for his slippers, he felt an ironical grimace flit briefly over his still-numb face. He was dragging himself from his slumbers in order to go to work at the Tabir Sarrail, the famous bureau of sleep, and dreams. To anyone else the paradox might have seemed wryly entertaining, but he was too anxious to smile outright.

A pleasant aroma of tea and toast floated up from downstairs. He knew both his mother and his old nurse were awaiting him eagerly, and he did his best to greet them with some show of warmth.

"Good morning, Mother! Good morning, Loke!"

"Good morning, Mark-Alem. Did you sleep well?"

There was a gleam of excitement in their eyes, connected, no doubt, with his new appointment. Perhaps, like himself not long before, they'd been thinking this was the last night when he'd enjoy the peaceful sleep of ordinary mortals. From now on his life was bound to be different.

As he ate his breakfast he couldn't concentrate his thoughts on anything, and his anxiety continued to grow. When he went upstairs to dress, instead of going back to his room he went into the big drawing room. The pale blue tones of the carpet had lost their power to soothe. He went over to the bookshelves and, just as he had done the day before in front of the medicine cabinet, stood for some time gazing at the titles on the spines of the books. Then he put out his hand and took down a heavy folio volume bound in dark-brown, almost black, leather. It was years since he'd last opened it. It contained the history of his family, and on the cover some unknown hand had inscribed the title, *The Quprilis from Generation to Generation,* followed by the French word, *Chronique.*

As he turned the pages he had difficulty following the lines of manuscript, the style of which varied with the different authors. It wasn't hard to guess that most of the writers had been old men, or else younger ones confronting the end of their lives or on the brink of some great misfortune—the sort of occasion when people feel an irresistible need to leave some testimony behind them.

The first of our great family to attain high office in the Empire was Meth Quprili, born some three hundred years ago in a small town in central Albania.

Mark-Alem heaved a deep sigh. His hand went on turning the pages, but his eyes paused only on the names of viziers and generals. Lord, they were all Quprilis! he thought. And when he woke up he'd been stupid enough to wonder at his own appointment! He really must be a prize idiot.

When he came upon the words *Palace of Dreams,* he realized he'd been trying both to find and to avoid them. But it was too late to skip to the next page.

Our family's connections with the Palace of Dreams have always been very complicated. At first, in the days of the Yildis Sarrail, *which dealt only with interpreting the stars, things were relatively simple. It was when the* Yildis Sarrail *became the* Tabir Sarrail *that they began to go wrong.* . . .

Mark-Alem's anxiety, which a short while ago had been distracted by all those names and titles, now seized him by the throat once more.

He started leafing through the *Chronicle* again, but this time roughly and fast, as though a gale had suddenly started to blow through the tips of his fingers.

Our patronymic is a translation of the Albanian word Ura (qyprija *or* kurpija); *it refers to a bridge*

> with three arches in central Albania, constructed
> in the days when the Albanians were still Chris-
> tians and built with a man walled up in its foun-
> dations. After the bridge, which he helped to
> build, was finished, one of our ancestors, whose
> first name was Gjon, followed an old custom and
> adopted the name of Ura, together with the stigma
> of murder attached to it.

Mark-Alem slammed the book shut and hurried from the
drawing room. A few moments later he was out in the
street.

It *was a* wet morning, with a light sleet falling. The tall
buildings, looking down on the bustle in the streets with their
heavy doors and wickets still shut, seemed to add to the
gloom.

Mark-Alem buttoned his overcoat right up to the neck. As
he glanced at the swirls of delicate flakes fluttering around the
wrought-iron streetlamps, he felt a cold shudder run down his
spine.

As usual at this hour of the day the avenue was full of clerks
from the ministries hurrying to get to their offices on time.
Mark-Alem wondered several times as he went along whether
he ought to have taken a cab. The Tabir Sarrail was farther
away than he'd thought, and a thin layer of half-melted snow
was making the pavements slippery.

He was now walking past the Central Bank. A little farther
on, a line of frost-covered carriages stood outside another
imposing building. He wondered which ministry it was.

Someone in front of him skidded on the pavement. Mark-
Alem watched him as he tried to recover his balance, fell,

picked himself up, examined—muttering an oath as he did so—first his bespattered cape and then the place on which he'd slipped, and finally continued on his way, somewhat dazed. Keep your eyes open! Mark-Alem said inwardly, not quite sure if he was warning the stranger or himself.

As a matter of fact, there was no need for him to worry. He hadn't been told to present himself at the office at any particular time; he wasn't even sure he had to be there in the morning. He suddenly realized he had no idea of the hours that were kept at the Tabir Sarrail.

Somewhere in the mist, away to his left, a clock let out a brazen chime, addressed as if to itself. Mark-Alem walked on faster. He'd already turned up his fur collar, but now involuntarily made as if to turn it up again. In fact, though, it wasn't his neck that was cold, but a specific place in his chest. He felt in the inside pocket of his jacket to make sure his letter of recommendation was still there.

He suddenly noticed there were fewer people about than before. All the clerks are in their offices already, he thought with a pang. But he soon calmed down; his position was quite different from theirs. He wasn't a civil servant yet.

In the distance he thought he could make out a wing of the Tabir Sarrail, and when he got nearer he found he was right. It really was the Palace, with its faded cupolas which looked as if they'd once been blue, or at least bluish, but which were now almost invisible through the sleet. This was one of the sides of the building. The front must face on to the street around the corner.

He crossed a small, almost deserted esplanade, over which rose the strangely slender minaret of a mosque. Yes, here was the entrance to the Palace. Its two wings stretched away into the mist, while the main part of the building stood back a little as if recoiling from some threat. Mark-Alem felt his anxiety increase. Before him lay a long series of identical entrances, but when he got nearer he realized that all these great doors, wet from the sleet, were closed, and looked as if they hadn't been opened for some time.

As he strolled by them, examining them out of the corner of his eye, a man with a cowl over his head suddenly materialized beside him.

"Which is the way in?" asked Mark-Alem.

The man pointed to the right. The sleeve of his cape was so ample it remained unaffected by the movement of the arm within, and his hand was dwarfed by the enormous folds of cloth. Good heavens, what a strange getup, thought Mark-Alem as he went in the direction indicated. After a while he heard more footsteps nearby. It was another hooded man.

"Over here," he said. "This is the staff entrance."

Mark-Alem, flattered at being taken for a member of staff, finally found the entrance. The doors looked very heavy. There were four of them, all exactly alike and fitted with heavy bronze knobs. He tried one of them and found it, strangely, lighter than he'd expected. He then found himself in a chilly corridor with a ceiling so high he felt as if he were at the bottom of a pit. On either side there was a long row of doors. He tried the handles of all of them until one opened, admitting him to another, less icy corridor. At last, beyond a glass partition, he saw some people. They were sitting in a circle, talking. They must be ushers or at least some kind of reception staff, for they were all wearing a sort of pale blue livery much the same color as the Palace cupolas. For a moment Mark-Alem thought he could see marks on their uniforms like those he'd noticed in the distance on the cupolas themselves and ascribed to damp. But he didn't have time to pursue his examination, for the people he was observing had stopped talking and were looking at him inquiringly. He

opened his mouth to greet them, but they were so obviously
annoyed at having their conversation interrupted that instead
of saying good morning he merely mentioned the name of the
official to whom he was supposed to present himself.

"Oh, it's about a job, is it?" said one of them. "First floor
on the right, door eleven!"

Like anyone entering a large government office for the first
time, but all the more so because he had arrived in a state of
numb uncertainty, Mark-Alem would have liked to exchange
a few words with someone. But these people seemed so
impatient to resume their confounded conversation he felt
they were actually ejecting him back into the corridor.

He heard a voice behind him: "Over there—on the
right!" Without looking around he walked on as directed.
Only the tension he was under and the cold shudders still
running through his body prevented him from feeling annoyed.

The corridor on the first floor was long and dark, with
dozens of doors opening off it, tall and unnumbered. He
counted ten and stopped outside the eleventh. He'd have
liked to make sure it really was the office of the person he was
looking for before he knocked, but the corridor was empty
and there was no one to ask. He drew a deep breath,
stretched out his hand, and gave a gentle tap. But no voice
could be heard from within. He looked first to his right, then
to his left, and knocked again, more loudly this time. Still no
answer. He knocked a third time and, still hearing nothing,
tried the door. Strangely enough it opened easily. He was
terrified, and made as if to close it again. He even put out his
hand to clutch it back as it creaked open wider still on its
hinges. Then he noticed the room was empty. He hesitated.
Should he go in? He couldn't think of any rule or custom that
applied to this situation. Finally the door stopped creaking.

He stood gazing wide-eyed at the benches lining the walls of the empty office. After lingering a moment in the doorway he felt for his letter of recommendation, and this restored his courage. He went in. Dash it all, he thought. Seeing in his mind's eye his large house in Royal Street and the influential relatives who often gathered there after dinner in the huge drawing room with its tall chimneypiece, he sat down on one of the benches with a comparatively casual air. Unfortunately, the image of his house and relatives soon faded, and he was once more seized with apprehension. He thought he detected a muffled sound like a whisper, but couldn't tell where it came from. Then, looking around the room he discovered a side door, from beyond which seemed to come the sound of voices. He sat still for a moment, straining his ears, but the murmur remained as indistinct as ever. By now his whole attention was concentrated on this door, on the other side of which he for some reason supposed it must be warmer.

He put his hands on his knees and sat like that for some time. At any rate he'd managed without too much trouble to get inside a building to which very few people had access. It was said even ministers themselves weren't allowed in without a special pass. Two or three times he glanced at the door where the sound of the voices came from, but he felt he could stay there for hours or even days without standing up and going over to open it. He'd just sit on the bench and wait, thanking his stars for letting him get as far as this anteroom. He hadn't expected it to be so easy. But had it really been as easy as all that? Then he reproached himself: a walk through the drizzle, a few closed doors, some ushers in copper-sulfate–colored liveries, this empty waiting room—you couldn't really call that difficult.

And yet, without quite knowing why, he heaved a sigh.

At that moment the door opened. He stood up. Someone

poked his head in, looked at him, then vanished again, leaving the door ajar. Inside, Mark-Alem heard him say: "There's someone out in the anteroom!"

Mark-Alem didn't know how long he waited. The door remained ajar, but instead of human voices he could now hear a strange crackling sound. The man he'd glimpsed before finally reappeared—a very short man holding a sheaf of papers which fortunately, as Mark-Alem said to himself, absorbed most of his attention. Nevertheless, he did dart a searching glance at Mark-Alem, who was tempted to offer some apology for having made him leave what was probably a nice warm office. But the midget's expression froze the words on Mark-Alem's lips. Instead, his hand slowly plucked the letter of recommendation from his pocket and held it out. The other seemed about to take it when he suddenly snatched back his arm as if afraid of being burned. He craned forward and scanned the letter for two or three seconds, then drew away. Mark-Alem thought he detected a mocking gleam in his eye.

"Come with me!" said the little man, heading for the door that led into the corridor.

Mark-Alem followed him out. At first he tried to memorize their route so as to be able to find his own way out, but he soon gave up the attempt as useless.

The corridor was even longer than it had seemed before. A faint light reached it from other passages branching off it. Mark-Alem and his guide finally turned along one of these. After a while the little man stopped in front of a door and went in, leaving it open for the visitor. Mark-Alem hesitated a moment, but when the other beckoned, he entered too.

Even before he felt the warmth he recognized the smell of red-hot coals coming from a big copper brazier in the middle of the room. A square-faced man with a morose expression was sitting at a wooden table. Mark-Alem had the feeling he'd been sitting waiting for them with his eyes fixed on the door before they'd even crossed the threshold.

The midget, with whom Mark-Alem reckoned he'd by now broken the ice, went over to the other man and whispered something in his ear. The man sitting at the table went on staring at the door as if someone were still knocking at it. He listened a moment longer to what the little man was saying, then muttered a few words himself, but in such a way that his face remained completely immobile. Mark-Alem began to think his enterprise was coming to nothing; that neither the letter of recommendation nor any of the other intercessions on his behalf carried any weight in those eyes, whose only interest seemed to reside in the door.

Then suddenly he heard himself being spoken to. His hand groped nervously inside his coat and brought out the letter of recommendation. But he immediately had the impression that he'd done the wrong thing and changed the atmosphere for the worse. For a split second he thought he must have misheard, but just as he was about to put the letter back in his pocket the midget reached out for the envelope. Mark-Alem, reassured, held it out nearer, but his relief was premature, for the other, as before, drew back and wouldn't touch the letter. Instead, he waved his hand in the air as if to indicate its proper destination. Mark-Alem, somewhat taken aback, realized he was supposed to hand the letter directly to the other official, who was no doubt superior in rank to his escort.

Rather to Mark-Alem's surprise, the senior civil servant actually took the letter. Even more amazingly, for the visitor had begun to think he would never take his eyes off the door, he opened the envelope and began to investigate its contents. Mark-Alem scrutinized him all the time he was reading in the hope of finding some clue in his face. But instead, something happened that he found really terrifying, filling him with the kind of faint but rapidly mounting panic that is often produced by an earthquake. And what Mark-Alem was feeling was indeed caused by a kind of upheaval. For as he read the letter, the official with the morose expression had slowly risen from his chair. The movement was so slow and so smooth it seemed to Mark-Alem that it would never end, and that the formidable official on whom his fate depended was going to turn into a monster of some kind before his very eyes. He was on the point of yelling, "Never mind! I don't want the job. Give me back my letter. I can't bear to watch you uncoiling like that!," when he saw that the process of standing was now over and the official was finally upright.

Mark-Alem was astonished, after all this, to find his host was of merely average height. He drew a deep breath, but once more his relief was premature. Now that he was standing, the official began to walk away from his desk at a pace as deliberate as before. He was making for the middle of the room. But the man who'd brought Mark-Alem here seemed unsurprised, and moved aside to let his superior pass. Now Mark-Alem felt quite reassured. The man must just be stretching his legs after sitting down for too long, or perhaps he suffered from piles, or gout. And to think, Mark-Alem said to himself, I nearly let out a howl of terror! My nerves really have been in a terrible state recently!

For the first time that morning he was able to face his interlocutor with his usual self-assurance. The official still had the letter of recommendation in his hand. Mark-Alem was expecting him to say, "Yes, I know all about it—the job's yours," or at least to give him some hope, make him some promise for the next few weeks or months. His many cousins wouldn't have exerted themselves for nothing, moving heaven and earth for over two months to arrange this appointment. And perhaps it was more important for this functionary, by whom he'd been so unnecessarily terrified, to remain on good terms with Mark-Alem's influential family than it was for Mark-Alem himself to get on the right side of *him*. As he watched him Mark-Alem was now so much at ease that for a moment he felt his face might break into a smile. And he'd have allowed it to do so if he hadn't suddenly been shattered by a new and horribly unexpected development. The official carefully folded up the letter of recommendation, and just as Mark-Alem was expecting some kindly comment, tore it across, twice. Mark-Alem shuddered. His lips moved as if to ask a question or perhaps just to get some air, but the official, as if he hadn't done enough already, went over and threw the pieces into the brazier. A mischievous flame spurted from the ash-choked embers, then died away leaving scraps of blackened paper.

"We don't accept recommendations at the Tabir Sarrail," said the official in a voice that reminded Mark-Alem of a clock chiming through the dark.

He was petrified. He didn't know what he ought to do—stay there, decamp without more ado, protest, or apologize. As if he had read his thoughts, the man who had brought him here silently left the room, leaving him alone with the official. They were now face-to-face, separated by the brazier. But this didn't last long. With the same interminable movement as before, the official moved back to his place behind the desk. But he didn't sit down. He merely cleared his throat as if preparing to deliver a speech, then, glancing back and forth between the door and Mark-Alem, said:

"We don't accept recommendations at the Tabir Sarrail. It's completely contrary to the spirit of this institution."

Mark-Alem didn't understand.

"The fundamental principle of the Tabir Sarrail resides not

in being open to outside influences but in remaining closed to them. Not in openness but in isolation. And so, not in recommendation but in its opposite. Nevertheless, from today you're appointed to work here.''

What's happening to me? thought Mark-Alem. His eyes, as if to make sure again of what had taken place, took in the remains of the letter, lying in ashes on the sleeping embers.

''Yes, from this moment on you work here,'' said the official again, having apparently noticed Mark-Alem's appalled expression.

He drew a deep breath, spread his hands out over the desk (which Mark-Alem now noticed was covered with files), and went on:

''The Tabir Sarrail or Palace of Dreams, as it's called in the language of today, is one of our great imperial State's most important institutions. . . .''

He was silent for a moment, scrutinizing Mark-Alem as if to assess how far he was capable of taking in the meaning of his words. Then he went on:

''The world has long recognized the importance of dreams, and the role they play in anticipating the fates of countries and of the people who govern them. You have certainly heard of the Oracle of Delphi in ancient Greece, and of the famous soothsayers of Rome, Assyria, Persia, Mongolia, and so on. Old books tell sometimes of the beneficial effects of the seers' predictions, sometimes of the penalties incurred by those who rejected them or accepted them too late. In short, books record all the events that have ever been told of in advance, whether or not they were actually affected by the forecast. Now this long tradition undoubtedly has its own importance, but it pales into insignificance beside the operations of the Tabir Sarrail. Our imperial State is the first in the history of the whole world to have institutionalized the interpretation of dreams, and so to have brought it to such a high degree of perfection.''

Mark-Alem listened in bewilderment. He still hadn't quite got over the previous emotions of the morning, and this matter-of-fact flood of abstruse phrases crowned all!

''The task of our Palace of Dreams, which was created directly by the reigning Sultan, is to classify and examine not the isolated dreams of certain individuals—such as those who in the past were for one reason or another granted the privilege, and who in practice enjoyed the monopoly, of prediction through interpretation of divine omens—but the 'Tabir' as a whole: in other words, all the dreams of all citizens without exception. This is a vast enterprise, beside which the oracles of Delphi and the predictions of all the hordes of prophets and magicians in the past are derisory. The idea behind the Sovereign's creation of the Tabir is that Allah looses a forewarning dream on the world as casually as He unleashes a flash of lightning or draws a rainbow or suddenly sends a comet close to us, drawn from the mysterious depths of the Universe. He dispatches a signal to the earth without bothering about where it will land; He is too far away to be concerned with such details. It is up to us to find out where the dream has come to earth—to flush it out from among millions, billions of others, as one might look for a pearl lost in the desert. For the interpretation of that dream, fallen like a stray spark into the brain of one out of millions of sleepers, may help to save the country or its Sovereign from disaster; may help to avert war or plague or to create new ideas.

''So the Palace of Dreams is no mere whim or fancy; it is one of the pillars of the State. It is here, better than in any surveys, statements, or reports compiled by inspectors, policemen, or governors of pashaliks, that the true state of the

Empire may be assessed. For in the nocturnal realm of sleep are to be found both the light and the darkness of humanity, its honey and its poison, its greatness and its vulnerability. All that is murky and harmful, or that will become so in a few years or centuries, makes its first appearance in men's dreams. Every passion or wicked thought, every affliction or crime, every rebellion or catastrophe necessarily casts its shadow before it long before it manifests itself in real life. It was for that reason that the Padishah decreed that no dream, not even one dreamed in the remotest part of the Empire on the most ordinary day by the most godforsaken creature, must fail to be examined by the Tabir Sarrail. And there's another imperial order that is still more fundamental: The table drawn up after the dreams of every day, week, and month have been collected, classified, and studied must always be absolutely accurate. To this end not only is there an enormous amount of work to be done in processing the raw material, but it is also of the utmost importance that the Tabir Sarrail should be closed to all external influence. For we know there are forces outside the Palace which for various reasons would like to infiltrate the Tabir Sarrail with their own agents, so that their own plans, ideas, and opinions might be presented as divine omens scattered by Allah among sleeping human brains. And that is why letters of recommendation are not allowed in the Tabir Sarrail.''

Mark-Alem's eyes involuntarily shifted to the burned paper now quivering on the embers.

"You'll be working in the Selection department," the official went on in the same tone as before. "You might have begun in one of the less important sections, as most new employees do, but you're going to begin in Selection because you suit us."

Mark-Alem glanced furtively at the quivering remains of

the letter, as if to say, "Haven't you gone yet?"

"And remember," said the other, "that what's expected of you above all is absolute secrecy. Never forget that the Tabir Sarrail is an institution totally closed to the outside world."

One of his hands rose from the table and wagged a menacing forefinger.

"Many, both individuals and whole factions, have tried to infiltrate us, but the Tabir Sarrail has never fallen into the trap. It stands alone and apart from human turmoil, outside all competing opinions and struggles for power, impervious to everything and without contacts with anyone. You may forget everything else I've just told you, but there's one thing, my boy, which, I repeat, you must always bear in mind. And that's secrecy. This isn't a piece of advice. It's the order of orders in the Tabir Sarrail. . . . And now, get to work. Ask in the corridor where the Selection department is. The people you're going to work with will have been told all about you before you get there. Good luck!"

Out in the corridor Mark-Alem was at a loss. There were no passersby from whom he might ask the way to Selection, so he started off at random. Scraps of what the senior official had said were still ringing in his ears. What's happening to me? he thought, shaking his head in an attempt to clear it. But instead of dispersing, the echoes of the words he'd just heard only clung to him all the more obstinately. He even had the impression that in this wilderness of corridors they ricocheted off the walls and colonnades, acquiring a resonance even more sinister than before: "You'll be working in Selection, because you suit us. . . ."

Without knowing why, Mark-Alem began to walk faster. "Selection." He kept repeating the word in his mind, and now he was alone it struck him as sounding very odd. He caught a glimpse of a figure a long way away down the corridor, but couldn't tell whether it was receding or approaching. He was tempted to call out to it, or at least wave, but it was much too far away. He walked faster still, almost ready to break into a run, shout, do anything so as to overtake the man who now seemed to him to represent his only chance of salvation in this endless corridor. As he hurried along he heard the sound of heavy footsteps somewhere to his left. He slowed down and listened. The footsteps, rhythmical and threatening, were coming from a side corridor opening into the main one. Mark-Alem turned and saw a group of men marching along silently, carrying large files. The covers of the files were the same color as the cupolas and the ushers' uniforms—pale blue with a tinge of green.

As the group passed him, Mark-Alem asked timidly, "Please, could you tell me how to get to Selection?"

"Go back the way you came," answered a hoarse voice. "I suppose you're new here?"

Mark-Alem had to wait for the other to get over a fit of coughing to be told that the fourth corridor on the right would take him to the stairs leading up to the second floor, and that he should ask for further instructions there.

"Thank you, sir," he said.

"Don't mention it," replied the stranger.

As he moved on, Mark-Alem heard him still coughing desperately and finally gasping, "I think I must have caught a cold."

It *took Mark-Alem* more than a quarter of an hour to find the Selection offices. The people there were waiting for him.

"I suppose you're Mark-Alem," said the first clerk he came across, before he'd had time to speak.

He nodded.

"Come with me," said the other. "The boss is waiting for you."

Mark-Alem followed obediently. They went through a series of rooms where dozens of clerks sat at long tables, poring over open files. None of them showed the slightest interest in either him or his guide, whose shoes clattered on the floor as he walked.

Like the others, the boss sat at a table with a couple of files open in front of him. The man escorting Mark-Alem went up to his superior and whispered something in his ear. But Mark-Alem had a feeling the boss hadn't heard. His eyes went on devouring the closely written pages in one of the files, yet Mark-Alem had a fleeting impression that on the edge of his glance there lurked, like a dying wave, the outer fringe of something fearful, though its epicenter was far away.

Mark-Alem hoped his escort would whisper to the boss again, but he showed no inclination to do so. He just stood there calmly, waiting for his superior to finish with the file.

He had to wait some time. It seemed to Mark-Alem as if the boss would never look up; as if he himself would be stuck there indefinitely, perhaps until office hours were over, or even longer. The whole room was plunged in silence. The only sound was the faint one made by the boss when he turned a page. At one point Mark-Alem noticed he'd stopped reading and was just staring vaguely at the file. He seemed to be thinking over what he'd just read. This went on for some time, perhaps for as long as the time he'd spent actually reading. Eventually the boss rubbed his eyes as if to remove one last mist from them, and looked up at Mark-Alem. The fearsome wave, which had already lost much of its force when Mark-Alem first saw it, had now completely disappeared.

"Are you the new one?"

Mark-Alem nodded. Without more ado the boss stood up and began to walk between the long tables. The other two followed. They went through several rooms which Mark-Alem sometimes did and sometimes didn't think he'd been through before.

When he saw a table in the distance with an unoccupied chair behind it and an unopened file on top, he realized this must be his place. And sure enough, the boss stopped and pointed at a spot between the table and the empty chair.

"That's where you'll be working," he said.

Mark-Alem looked at the unopened file with its bluish cover.

"The Selection service occupies several rooms like this," said the boss with a sweep of his arm. "It's one of the most important departments in the Tabir Sarrail. Some people think Interpretation is *the* essential department. But it isn't. The interpreters like to think they're the aristocrats of this institution, and affect to look down on us selectors. But as you must know, this is pure vanity on their part. Anyone with the least gumption can see that without us here in Selection, Interpretation would be like a mill without any wheat. We're the ones who supply them with all their raw material. We are the basis of their success."

He waved a dismissive hand.

"Oh well . . . You'll be working here, so you'll see for yourself. I believe you've already been given the necessary instructions. I don't want to overwhelm you on your first day, so I shan't go into detail now about all your duties. I'll just tell you what you need to know to start with, and you can pick up the rest as you go along. This is the chief room in Selection."

Another of the sweeping gestures.

"Between ourselves, we call it the Lentil Room, because

this is where the dreams are first sifted. In other words, this is where it all starts. Here in this very room . . ."

He blinked as if he'd lost the thread of what he'd been saying.

"Well," he went on after a moment, "to be quite accurate I ought to say the first sifting is done by our provincial sections. There are about nineteen hundred of them all over the Empire. Each one has its own subsections, and all these cells do a preliminary sorting before they send the dreams to the Center. But the sorting they do is only provisional. The real selection begins here. Just as the farmer separates the wheat from the chaff, so we separate the dreams that contain something of interest from those that do not. It's this winnowing process that is the essence of our Selection. Do you see?"

The boss's eyes were growing brighter and brighter. His words, which had come with difficulty before, now crowded on him faster than he could formulate his ideas, and he kept speaking faster and faster as if to try to make use of them all.

"Yes, that's the principal aim of our work," he repeated, "to eliminate from the files any dreams that are devoid of interest. To begin with, all those that are purely private and have nothing to do with the State. Then dreams caused by hunger or satiety, cold or heat, illness and so on—in short, all those that are connected with the flesh. Then come the sham dreams, those that never really happened but have been invented by people to further their ambitions, or by mythomaniacs or provocateurs. All these three categories have to be weeded out. But that's easily said! It isn't so easy actually to identify them. A dream may seem to be purely personal, or due to trivial causes like hunger or rheumatism, when in fact it's directly relevant to matters of State—probably more so than the latest speech by some member of the government!

But to recognize that takes experience and maturity. One error of judgment and everything can start to go wrong, do you see? To cut a long story short, ours is very highly skilled work.''

He now abandoned irony and adopted a more easy tone to explain to Mark-Alem what his practical duties would be. There was still a trace in his eyes, however, of previous tension.

"As you'll have noticed," he went on, "there are other rooms beside this one, and in order to get a better idea of the work you'll be called upon to do you must spend a day or two in each of them. Then, when you've acquired an overall idea of what Selection is, you'll come back here to the Lentil Room, where you'll find the work all the easier because of your initiation. But that won't begin until next week. Meanwhile, you'll make a start here."

He leaned across the table, drew the file over and flipped open its blue cover.

"This is your first file. It contains a group of dreams that arrived on October nineteenth. Read them very carefully, but whatever you do don't be too hasty. If you think there's the slightest chance that a dream might have been fabricated, leave it where it is and don't be in too much of a hurry to remove it. After you there'll be another sorter, or, to give him his proper title, a second inspector, and he'll check what you've done and correct any errors. Then there's another inspector to check up on him, and so on. In fact, all the people you see in this room are doing just that. So good luck!"

He stayed there another few seconds looking at Mark-Alem, then turned around and left. Mark-Alem was momentarily rooted to the spot, then slowly, trying not to make any noise, he edged the chair back a little, slid between it and the table, and, still very cautiously, sat down.

The file now lay open in front of him. His wish, and that of his family, had been granted. He'd been given a job in the Tabir Sarrail; he was even sitting on a chair at his desk, a genuine official in the mysterious Palace.

He bent a little closer over the file, until his eyes could make out what was written in it, then calmly began to read. The stiff first page bore the name and date of the file, followed lower down by the inscription *Issued to Surkurlah. Contains 63 dreams.*

With an apprehensive finger Mark-Alem turned to the next page. This, unlike the first, was covered with closely written text. The first three lines were slightly separated from the rest and underlined in green ink. They read: *Dream of Yussuf, clerk in the post office at Aladjehisar, subprefecture of Kerk-Kili, pashalik of Kustendil, last September 3 just before dawn.*

Mark-Alem looked up from the file. September 3, he thought bemusedly. Could it all be true? Was he really now an official in the Tabir Sarrail, installed at his own desk and reading the dream of Yussuf, who worked at the post office in Aladjehisar in the subprefecture of Kerk-Kili in the pashalik of Kustendil—reading it in order to settle his fate, to decide whether his dream was to be thrown in the wastepaper basket or inserted into and analyzed by the vast machinery of the Tabir?

He felt a quiver of pleasure run up his spine. Looking down at the file again he read: *Three white foxes on the minaret of the local mosque . . .*

Suddenly he was startled by the ringing of a bell. He looked up sharply as if he'd been tapped on the shoulder. Looking first to his left and then to his right, he was amazed by what he saw. All the people who had hitherto seemed glued to their chairs and mesmerized by the files open in front of them had suddenly broken the spell. They were now standing up, chatting and scraping their chairs on the floor as the bell went on echoing through the rooms.

"What is it?" asked Mark-Alem. "What's going on?"

"It's the morning break," answered his nearest neighbor. (But where had he been until now?) "The morning break," he repeated. "Of course you're new, so you don't know the timetable. But you'll soon learn."

On all sides the occupants of the room were moving between the long tables and making for the door. Mark-Alem did his best to go on reading, but it was impossible: others kept jostling him and knocking against his chair. But despite all this he bent over the file again, attracted to it now as by a magnet. *Three white foxes . . .* Then he heard a voice speaking just by his ear:

"You can get coffee and *salep* downstairs. Come on, there's bound to be something you like."

Mark-Alem scarcely had time to see what the speaker looked like, but he got up, closed the file, and followed everyone else to the door.

Out in the corridor he had no need to ask the way. Everybody was going in the same direction. Those in the main corridor were joined by an endless stream of others from the side corridors. Mark-Alem mingled in the human tide, now advancing shoulder to shoulder. He was impressed by the number of people employed in the Tabir Sarrail. There were hundreds of them, perhaps thousands.

The sound of footsteps grew louder, especially on the stairs. After descending one flight they went down a long straight corridor, then down another lot of stairs. Mark-Alem noticed that the windows grew narrower on every landing. It seemed to him they must be heading for some kind of basement. By now all the people were crowded together in one mass. He could make out the separate scents of coffee and *salep* even before they got to the refreshment room. It reminded him of breakfast in their own big house. He was filled with another wave of delight. In the distance he could see long counters with dozens of assistants handing out steaming bowls of *salep* and cups of coffee. He let himself be swept toward the counters. Amid the general hubbub you could hear people sipping their coffee or herb tea, brief bursts of coughing, the clink of coins. A lot of these people seemed to have colds, unless after being silent for hours on end they needed to clear their throats before starting to speak.

After being pressed into a queue, Mark-Alem found himself stuck near a counter, unable to move either forward or back. He realized other people were pushing in front of him, reaching over his head to take cups or pay for them, but he was determined not to let it bother him. Anyhow, he didn't really want anything to eat or drink. He stayed where he was, shunted back and forth by the crowd, his only concern to do the same as everyone else.

"If you don't move yourself you won't get anything to drink!" said a voice behind him. "You might let me through, at any rate!"

Mark-Alem made way at once. The person who'd spoken, apparently surprised by his eagerness to oblige, looked round curiously. He had a long ruddy face with nice round cheeks. He stared at Mark-Alem for a moment.

"Have you just been taken on?"

Mark-Alem nodded.

"Yes, that's obvious."

He took another couple of steps toward the counter, then turned and said, "What'll you have? Coffee or *salep*?"

Mark-Alem was tempted to say, "Nothing, thanks," but that might have seemed odd. And wasn't he supposed to be trying to be like everyone else and not draw attention to himself?

"A coffee," he whispered, but moving his lips enough for the other to understand what he was saying.

He felt in his pocket for some change, but meanwhile his new acquaintance had turned around again and reached the counter. Mark-Alem, waiting, couldn't help hearing snatches of the conversations going on around him. They were like fragments being ground up by some great millstone. But now and then a few audible words or even whole sentences would escape briefly, no doubt to be crushed at the next turn of the wheel. Mark-Alem strained his ears to listen and was astonished at what he heard. These people weren't talking about the Tabir Sarrail at all, but about the most trivial and ordinary things, such as the cold weather, the quality of the coffee, the races, the national lottery, the flu epidemic in the capital. Not a single word about what went on in this building. You'd have thought they were officials in the Land Office or some ordinary ministry, not that they worked in the famous Palace of Dreams, the most mysterious institution in the whole Empire.

Mark-Alem saw his new friend emerging from the crush, a cup of coffee balanced precariously in either hand.

"This queueing—what a bore!" he said, still holding on to both cups as he tried to steer a way to a table that was free among the scores or even hundreds scattered around the room. No chairs were provided, and the tabletops were bare. They served merely as ledges to lean on, and a place to leave empty cups.

The other man finally found a free table and set down the coffees. Mark-Alem shyly offered the coins he'd been holding in his hand. The other waved them away.

"It's nothing," he said.

"Thank you!"

Mark-Alem picked up a cup of coffee, still clutching the money in his other hand.

"When did you start?" asked his companion.

"Today."

"Really? Congratulations! Well, you're right to . . ." He let the sentence trail off and took a sip of coffee. "What section are you in?"

"Selection."

"Selection?" the other exclaimed, as if surprised. He smiled. "Well, you've certainly made a good start. People usually begin their career in Reception, or even lower down, in the copying section."

Mark-Alem suddenly wanted to find out more about the Tabir Sarrail. A small chink had appeared in his former reticence.

"So Selection's an important department, is it?" he asked.

The other stared at him.

"Yes, very important. Especially for a young recruit . . ."

"How do you mean?"

"I mean especially for someone who's just been appointed."

"And what about in general? Not just for someone young, but in general?"

"Yes, of course. In general it's regarded as a crucial department. Of the utmost significance."

Now it was Mark-Alem's turn to stare.

"Naturally there *are* sections that are more important still. . . ."

"Interpretation, for instance?"

The other lowered his cup.

"Well, well—you're not such a novice as you seem," he

said with a smile. "You've learned quite a lot already, considering it's your first day!"

Mark-Alem was tempted to smile back, but realized it was too soon to make so bold. The icy carapace that seemed to cover his face this extraordinary morning hadn't quite melted yet.

"Of course, Interpretation is the very essence of the Tabir Sarrail," the other went on. "Its nerve center, its brain, so to speak, for it's there that the preliminaries carried out in the other sections take on their real significance. . . ."

Mark-Alem listened feverishly.

"And the people who work there are known as the aristocrats of the Tabir?"

His companion pursed his lips and thought for a moment.

"Yes. Something like that. Although of course . . ."

"What?"

"Don't go thinking there aren't any others above them."

"And who are they?" asked Mark-Alem, surprised at his own audacity.

The other looked back at him calmly.

"The Tabir Sarrail is always bigger than it seems," he said.

Mark-Alem would have liked to ask him what he meant, but was afraid of presuming too far.

"In addition to the ordinary Tabir," went on the other, "there's the secret Tabir. The dreams that are analyzed there are not sent in by people themselves—they're obtained by the State through methods and means of its own. You'll appreciate that *that's* a section no less important than Interpretation!"

"Of course," replied Mark-Alem, "although . . ."

"Although what?"

"Don't all the dreams, whether they're sent in spontaneously or collected by the secret Tabir, end up in Interpretation?"

"As a matter of fact, all the sections but one are duplicated—they all have offices both in the ordinary Tabir and in the secret one. Only the Interpretation department is a single service common to both. However, that doesn't mean it's superior in the hierarchy to the secret Tabir as such."

"But perhaps it's not inferior either?"

"Perhaps. There's a certain amount of rivalry between them."

"In short, both those sections constitute the aristocracy of the Tabir."

The other man smiled.

"More or less, if that's how you like to put it."

He took another swig at his cup, though there was no coffee left in it now.

"But you mustn't suppose *even they* are at the top," he went on. "There are others again above them."

Mark-Alem looked at him hard to see if he was serious.

"And who are they?"

"The Master-Dream officers."

"What?"

"The Master-Dream officers. The section that deals with the Arch-Dream, as they've taken to calling it lately."

"And what's that?"

The other lowered his voice.

"We probably oughtn't to be talking about that sort of thing," he said. "But after all, you *have* just become a member of staff. And these are really only organizational matters—I don't suppose there's anything secret about them."

"Probably not," said Mark-Alem.

He couldn't wait to find out more.

"Do go on," he said encouragingly. "I do belong here, in a way. My mother belongs to the Quprili family."

"The Quprili family!"

Mark-Alem wasn't surprised by his interlocutor's astonishment. He was used to meeting with this reaction whenever anyone found out about his origins.

"As soon as you said you'd gone straight into Selection, I guessed you must belong to a family close to the State. But I must admit I didn't imagine those dizzy heights."

"Quprili was my mother's maiden name," said Mark-Alem. "My own name's different."

"That makes no odds. It's the same thing for all intents and purposes."

Mark-Alem looked at him.

"Tell me some more about the Master-Dream."

His companion drew a deep breath. Then, as if sensing his voice wasn't going to be loud enough to need all that air, he exhaled some of it again before he spoke.

"As perhaps you know, every Friday a traditional ceremony is held, ancient but discreet, in which one dream, selected as the most important of all the thousands we've received and analyzed during the previous week, is presented to the Sultan. That's the Master- or Arch-Dream."

"I have heard of it, but only vaguely, as a kind of legend."

"Well, it's not a legend—it's a fact. And it gives work to hundreds of people in the Master-Dream department."

He looked at Mark-Alem for some time before going on.

"And—would you believe it?—a dream like that, with its significant omens, is sometimes more useful to the Sovereign than a whole army of soldiers or all his diplomats put together."

Mark-Alem listened openmouthed.

"So now do you see why the position of the Master-Dream officers is so superior to ours?"

What a gigantic mechanism, thought Mark-Alem. Yes, the Tabir Sarrail really was unimaginably vast.

"You never see any of them about," the other went on. "They even have their coffee and *salep* in a place of their own."

"A place of their own . . ." Mark-Alem echoed.

His new friend had just opened his mouth to supply more information when the sound of a bell, the same one as had announced the coffee break, put a sudden stop to everything that was going on around them.

Mark-Alem had neither time nor need to ask what it meant. Even before the ringing had stopped, everyone started to rush for the exits. Those who hadn't finished the drinks in front of them emptied their cups and glasses in one gulp. Others, who'd only just been served with beverages still too hot to drink, just abandoned them and made off like the rest. Mark-Alem's companion had fallen silent just as suddenly, then nodded curtly and turned away. Mark-Alem would have tried to detain him and ask him one last question, but as he was about to do so he was jostled first to the left and then to the right, and so lost sight of him.

As he let himself be swept out along with the crowd, he realized he'd forgotten to ask his new acquaintance his name. If only I knew what section he works in, he sighed. Then he consoled himself with the thought that they might meet again at the next day's coffee break and be able to have another chat.

The crowd was thinning by now, and Mark-Alem tried to find one of the faces he'd seen before in the Selection department. In vain. He had to ask the way back there twice. When he arrived he crept in quietly, trying not to be noticed. The last chairs were still being scraped into place. Nearly all the clerks were ensconced at their long tables again. Mark-Alem tiptoed to his desk, drew out his chair, and sat down. He did nothing for a few moments, then bent over his file and started to read: *Three white foxes on the minaret of the local mosque* . . . then suddenly he looked up. He felt as if someone were hailing him from a long way away, sending out some strange, faint, doleful signal like a call for help or a sob. What is it? he wondered. The question soon absorbed him absolutely. Without knowing why, he looked at the high windows. It was the first time he'd done so. Beyond the windowpanes the rain, so familiar but now so distant, mingled as it fell with delicate flakes of snow. The flakes eddied wildly in the morning light, now distant too—so far away it seemed to belong to another life, another world from which perhaps that ultimate signal had been sent out to him.

With a vague sense of guilt he looked away and bent over his file. But before he started reading again he heaved a deep sigh: Oh, God!

SELECTION

...

ii.

It was a Tuesday afternoon.

The offices would be stopping work in an hour. Mark-Alem looked up from his papers and rubbed his eyes. He'd started this job a week ago, but he still hadn't got used to so much reading. His right-hand neighbor fidgeted about on his chair, but went on reading. From the whole length of the long table came the regular rustle of turned pages. All the clerks had their eyes glued to their files.

It was November. The files were getting thicker and

thicker. The flow of dreams tended to increase at this time of year. That was one of the main things Mark-Alem had noticed during his first week. People would go on having dreams and sending them in for ever and ever, but they varied in number from season to season. And this was one of the busy periods. Tens of thousands of dreams were arriving from all over the Empire, and would go on doing so at the same rate until the end of the year. The files would swell as the weather grew colder. Then, after the New Year, things would slacken off until spring.

Mark-Alem gave another surreptitious glance at his right-hand neighbor, then shot a look at the one on the left. Were they really reading or merely pretending? He leaned his head on his hand and looked down at the page in front of him, but instead of letters he seemed to see only spidery scrawls against a background of gray. No, he couldn't go on reading. Many of the others poring over their files were probably only shamming. It really was an awful job.

As he sat with his brow propped on his palm, he remembered what the older hands in Selection had been telling him that week about the ebb and flow of dreams, and the way their numbers varied according to time of year, rainfall, temperature, atmospheric pressure, and humidity. The veterans of the department were experts on this sort of thing. They knew all about the influence of snow, wind, and lightning on the quantity of dreams, not to mention the effect of earthquakes, comets, and eclipses of the moon. Some people in the department were probably real adepts in the analysis of dreams, genuine scientists who could detect strange hidden significances in visions that to the ordinary eye seemed like meaningless mental doodlings. And in no other department in the Tabir Sarrail could you find old campaigners like those in Selection, able to foretell the size of the crop of dreams as

easily as ordinary graybeards could predict bad weather from
their rheumatics.

Suddenly Mark-Alem thought of the man he'd met on his
first day. Where was he? For several days Mark-Alem had
looked for him among the crowd of clerks in the coffee break,
but he'd never seen him anywhere. Perhaps he's not well, he
thought. Or he might have been sent on an assignment to
some distant province. He might be one of the Tabir's inspectors, who spent most of their time away on official missions;
or he might be just an ordinary messenger.

Mark-Alem imagined the thousands of Tabir Sarrail offices
scattered all over the vast country—the makeshift buildings,
sometimes mere shacks, housing them and their even more
modest staff. This usually consisted of two or three hard-
worked, ill-paid clerks ready to bow to the ground before the
meanest courier from the Tabir when he came to collect the
dreams, stammering and stuttering and crawling to him just
because he represented the Center. In some remote areas the
inhabitants of subprefectures would set out before dawn and
trudge through the rain and mud to relate their dreams in
these dismal little offices. They'd bellow from outside, not
bothering to knock at the door: "Are you open yet, Hadji?"

Most of them couldn't read or write, so they came very
early in the day so as not to forget their dreams, not even
stopping for a drink at a nearby tavern. Each one would tell
his story to a drowsy-eyed copyist who cursed both the dream
and the dreamer. "God grant us better luck this time!" some
would say when they'd finished. There was a time-honored
legend about some poor wretch who lived in a forgotten
byway and whose dream saved the State from a terrible
calamity. As a reward the Sovereign summoned him to the
capital, received him in his palace, told him to take his choice
among the royal treasures, and even offered him one of his

nieces in marriage. And so on. "God grant . . ." the yokels would repeat as they set off through the mud again, most of them probably heading for the tavern. The copyist would watch them go sardonically, and before they disappeared around the bend in the road, he would mark their dreams "Useless."

Despite strict instructions that they should judge dreams completely impartially and without prejudice, this was how the clerks carried out the first selection. The local inhabitants were an open book to them. Even before a new arrival crossed the threshold of their office they knew whether he was a hellraiser, a drunk, a layabout, or suffered from an ulcer. This attitude had often caused problems, and a few years before it had been decided that the first sifting should no longer be entrusted to the local offices. But the ensuing flood of dreams converging on central Selection was so great the decision had to be revoked, and the first sifting continued to be done locally for want of a better solution.

Naturally the dreamers themselves knew nothing of all this. Every so often they would come to the door and ask, "Well, Hadji, any answer about my dream?"

"No, not yet," replied Hadji. "Patience, Abdul Kader! The Empire's a big place, and even though they work day and night the central office can't keep up with all the dreams they're sent."

"Yes, of course. You're right," the other would answer, gazing at the horizon in the direction where he imagined the Center to be. "How can we know anything about affairs of State?" And he'd clump off in his clogs to the pothouse.

Mark-Alem had learned all this the morning before from an inspector at the Tabir with whom he'd had coffee. The inspector was just back from a distant Asian province and was about to set out again for the European part of the Empire. What

he said took Mark-Alem aback. Could everything really begin
in so humble a manner? But the inspector, as if sensing his
disappointment, hastened to explain that it wasn't like that
everywhere. Some local sections were in solid buildings in
imposing cities in Asia and Europe, and those who brought
their dreams there were not poor yokels but distinguished
people loaded down with honors and titles and university
degrees—people of wit, intelligence, and ambition. The inspector expatiated for a while on this point, and Mark-Alem's
image of the Tabir Sarrail gradually regained its former luster.
The inspector was just launching into an account of some
other episodes in his travels when the bell interrupted him;
and now Mark-Alem was trying to imagine the rest for himself. He thought of the peoples who lived on the left side of
the Empire and of those who lived on the right; of those who
had many dreams and those who had few; of those who were
quite ready to tell their dreams and those, like the Albanians,
who were very reserved about them (Mark-Alem set great
store by his Albanian origins and automatically registered
anything that concerned Albania). He thought of the dreams
dreamed by peoples in a state of revolt, by peoples who'd
been the victims of cruel massacres, by peoples who suffered
from periods of insomnia. The latter were a source of special
anxiety to the State, since after a latent period a sudden
resurgence was to be expected. So special measures were
taken in advance to deal with it.

When his informant had spoken of whole peoples suffering
from insomnia, Mark-Alem had looked at him in astonishment.

"I know it may strike you as strange," said the other, "but
it has to be understood relatively. A people is deemed to be
suffering from insomnia when its total amount of sleep de-
scends appreciably below the norm. And where is anyone in

a better position to assess this difference than in the Tabir Sarrail?''

"Of course,'' agreed Mark-Alem. He remembered his own recent sleepless nights, though he quickly told himself the sleeplessness of a whole nation must be very different from that of an individual.

He started glancing covertly again to right and left. All the other members of staff seemed to be deep in their papers, as spellbound as if the files, instead of consisting merely of written pages, were braziers giving off intoxicating fumes. Perhaps I'll gradually succumb to that fascination too, thought Mark-Alem morosely, and end up forgetting all about the world and the human race.

In the past week, in accordance with his boss's directive, he'd spent half a day with an elderly clerk in each of the rooms belonging to Selection, so as to familiarize himself with every aspect of the work and acquire some experience. Then, two days ago, when he'd finished his tour of all the operations, he'd come back to the desk that was allocated to him on the day he was first appointed.

His peregrinations from one room to another had given Mark-Alem a general view of the way the Selection department worked. After the first scrutiny in the Lentil Room, the dreams rejected as valueless were done up in big bundles and sent to Archives, while those that were retained were divided into groups according to the subjects they were related to. The groups were: security of the Empire and of the Sovereign (plots, acts of treachery, rebellions); domestic politics (first and foremost the unity of the Empire); foreign politics (alliances and wars); law and order (extortion, injustice, corruption); signs of a Master-Dream; and miscellaneous.

The sorting of dreams into divisions and subdivisions was no easy matter. There had been long discussions as to whether the task should be entrusted to Selection or to Interpretation. It would have gone to Interpretation if that section hadn't been so overworked already. Finally a compromise solution was found: Selection was to classify the dreams, but only in a tentative and preliminary way. So each file was headed not "Dreams concerned with such and such a subject" but "Dreams possibly concerning such and such a subject." Furthermore, while Selection bore the entire responsibility for dividing dreams into those that were useless and those that were of interest, it had no responsibility at all concerning any further classification. Which meant that Selection dealt essentially with basic sorting. Sorting was the *raison d'être* of Selection, and interpretation the *raison d'être* of the Tabir Sarrail as a whole.

"So now you understand that we're the ones who control all the incoming material," said the head of his section to Mark-Alem, the day he came back to his original desk. "At first you probably thought that because the work in Selection is primarily sorting, and because we appointed you to this section right away, it was the least important operation in the Tabir. But I imagine you see now that it's the basis of everything that's done here. So we never assign beginners to this section, and we only made an exception for you because you suit us."

"You suit us . . ." Mark-Alem had pondered the phrase again and again to try to puzzle out what it meant. But it remained as enigmatic and impenetrable as ever, like a wall so smooth and hard you couldn't get any purchase to climb over it.

He rubbed his eyes again and tried to get on with his reading. But he couldn't. The characters looked all red now, as if reflecting fire or blood.

He'd put aside forty or so dreams that he judged to be

devoid of interest. Most of them seemed to have their origin in everyday worries, while others looked as if they were hoaxes. But he wasn't quite sure; he'd better read them again. As a matter of fact he'd already read each of them two or three times; but he still didn't trust his own judgment. The head of the section had told him that when in doubt about a dream he should put a big question mark against it and pass it on to the next sorter. But he'd already done this quite often. In fact, he'd rejected hardly any dreams as useless, and if he didn't keep back the present batch his boss might think he was afraid to take risks and unloaded everything on his colleagues. But he was supposed to be a sorter, employed to make choices, not to shift the responsibility off onto others. What would happen if all the sorters shirked like that and sent almost all the dreams on to Interpretation? Interpretation would eventually refuse to take them, and probably complain to Administration. And Administration would inquire into what had gone wrong.

"A fine mess I'm in," sighed Mark-Alem. "But what the hell!"

And hastily, as if he were afraid he might change his mind, he scribbled "Useless," followed by his initials, at the top of four or five pages. As he was doing the same with the pages that came after, he felt a kind of vengeful joy directed against all the unknown wretches with their stomachaches and their piles who'd been tormenting him for the whole of the past couple of days with their stupid dreams—which they probably hadn't even dreamed at all, but only heard about from other people.

"Idiots, asses, impostors," he muttered as he wrote the fatal formula.

But his hand moved ever more slowly, until finally it just hung poised over the paper.

Hold on a bit, he told himself. What's the point of losing your temper?

And in less than a minute his rage had been replaced by doubt again.

When you came right down to it, this job was by no means easy, and these unknown wretches could even get you into trouble. The staff of every department trembled at the mere thought of Investigation being called in. Mark-Alem had been told about one occasion when some out-of-the-way event had occurred and a dreamer wrote in to the Tabir Sarrail to claim he'd foreseen it in a dream. In such cases a dream was traced by means of the registration number that had been assigned to it in Reception, then taken out of the Archives and checked, and if the complaint was well-founded, a search was instituted to find the people responsible for overlooking or disregarding the warning. The guilty parties might be interpreters, but they might equally well be sorters who'd rejected the dream as useless—an even more heinous fault, since there was more excuse for an interpreter who misread a sign than for a sorter who missed it altogether.

To hell with all of it! thought Mark-Alem, surprising himself with this spark of rebelliousness. What does it matter, anyway!

He wrote "Useless" on another page, then hesitated again over the next. Automatically, not knowing what to do with the piece of paper still in front of him, he began to reread it: *A piece of wasteland by a bridge; the sort of vacant lot where people throw rubbish. Among all the trash and dust and bits of broken lavatory, a curious musical instrument playing all by itself, except for a bull that seems to be maddened by the sound and is standing by the bridge and bellowing . . .*

Must be an artist, thought Mark-Alem. Some embittered out-of-work musician.

And he started to write "Useless" on the page. But hardly had he begun when his eye was caught by some earlier lines which he'd skipped before, and which recorded the name of the dreamer, his profession, and the date when he'd had the dream. Strangely enough he wasn't a musician—he was a street trader who had a market stall in the capital. Lord! said Mark-Alem to himself, unable to take his eyes off this information. A beastly greengrocer, crawling out of his hovel just to make life difficult for you! . . . What's more, he lived in the capital, so it would be easier for him to make a complaint if the situation arose. Mark-Alem carefully erased what he'd just written and put the page among the dreams that he'd classified as of possible interest. "Think yourself lucky, idiot!" he murmured, casting a last glance at the page as at someone he'd done an undeserved favor. He dipped his pen in the ink, and without even rereading them, marked a few more pages as "Useless." His anger had now evaporated and he went on more calmly. He still had eight dreams to deal with out of those he'd at first sight dismissed as worthless. He studied them soberly one after the other and, with the exception of one that he put among the "Of interest" pile, left all the rest where they were. You didn't need to be an expert to guess that they all originated in family squabbles, constipation, or enforced chastity.

Would these office hours never end? His eyes were beginning to smart again, but he got out a few more as-yet-unexamined pages from the file and spread them in front of him. Pretending to read them, he thought, was even more tiring than really doing so. He selected the pages with the least writing on them, and read one of them without bothering to look at the name of the dreamer: *A black cat with a*

*moon in its teeth was running along pursued by a mob
of people, leaving a trail of blood from the wounded
moon in its wake. . . .*

Yes, this dream was worth looking into. Mark-Alem read
it again before including it among the dreams that were of
interest. This really was a serious dream which it would be a
pleasure to analyze. It made him think that the work of the
interpreters, difficult though it might be, must be very interesting, especially when they had to deal with such examples
as this. Even he, despite his weariness, felt the beginnings of
an inclination to interpret it. Not that it was very difficult.
Given that the moon was a symbol of the State and of religion,
the black cat must represent some force that was hostile to
them. A dream like this, thought Mark-Alem, might easily be
proclaimed a Master-Dream. He looked at the dreamer's
address. He lived in a town on the European borders of the
Empire. That was where all the best dreams came from, he
noticed. When he'd reread it a third time, it struck him as
even more attractive and meaningful than before. Of particular interest was the crowd, which would no doubt catch the
black cat and get the moon out of its clutches. Yes, this dream
would certainly be recognized one day as a Master-Dream, he
thought. As he contemplated the sheet of ordinary paper it
was written on, he smiled as someone might smile on an
unassuming young girl he knew was destined to become a
princess.

Mark-Alem now felt strangely relieved. He thought for a
moment of reading another two or three pages, then decided
not to. He didn't want to blunt the edge of his satisfaction.
He turned and looked at the great windows, beyond which
dusk was now falling. He wouldn't examine any more dreams
today. He'd just wait for the bell to ring, announcing the end
of the working day. Although the daylight was now fading

fast, the heads of all the other clerks were still bent over their files. It was clear they'd never look up before the bell rang even if the room was swallowed up in eternal night.

In the end the bell did ring. Mark-Alem hastily collected his papers. There was a din as every drawer in the room was opened and every file stowed away. Mark-Alem locked the drawer in his own desk. Although he was among the first to leave the room, it took him a good quarter of an hour to get right out of the building.

It was cold out in the street. The staff poured out of the doorways in groups, then dispersed in different directions. As they did every evening, a crowd of onlookers watched from the pavement opposite as the people who worked in the Palace of Dreams emerged. Out of all the great State institutions, not excluding the Palace of the Sheikh-ul-Islam and the offices of the Grand Vizier, the Tabir Sarrail was the only one that aroused public curiosity. So much so that almost no day went by without hundreds of people gathering to stand and wait for the staff to go home. Silently, with their collars turned up against the cold, they observed the mysterious officials who were entrusted with the State's most mysterious work. They gazed at them intently, as if trying to read in their faces the dreams it was their task to decipher. The crowd didn't go away until the heavy doors of the great Palace had creaked shut.

Mark-Alem began to hurry. The streetlamps weren't lighted yet, but they would be by the time he reached the street where he lived. Ever since he'd started working in the Tabir Sarrail, darkness had made him feel apprehensive.

The streets were full of pedestrians, and every so often carriages dashed by with drawn curtains. Mark-Alem thought they must be taking beautiful courtesans to secret rendezvous, and heaved a sigh.

When he got to his own street the lamps had indeed been lighted. It was a quiet residential street; half of the houses were surrounded by heavy wrought-iron railings. The chestnut sellers were getting ready to go home. Some had already packed away their chestnuts, paper cones, and coal, and looked as though they were waiting for their braziers and the wire sieves on top to cool down. The policeman on duty saluted Mark-Alem respectfully. A neighbor, Betch Bey, a former army officer, came out of the corner café, dead drunk, with a couple of friends. He whispered something to the others when he saw Mark-Alem, who as he passed them sensed their eyes resting on him with a mixture of curiosity and fear. He walked on faster. He could see from a distance that the lights were on in the ground floor and second floor of the house. There must be visitors, he thought, but couldn't repress a shudder. As he got nearer he could see a carriage drawn up outside the gate with the letter Q for Quprili carved on both doors. But instead of reassuring him, this only added to his uneasiness.

Loke, the old servant, came and opened the gate for him.

"What's going on?" he said, nodding toward the lighted windows upstairs.

"Your uncles have come to see you."

"Has anything happened?"

"No. They're just visiting."

Mark-Alem sighed with relief.

What's the matter with me? he wondered as he went through the courtyard to the front door. Often, coming home very late, he'd felt worried when he saw lights in the windows, but he'd never been as troubled as this evening. It must be my new job, he thought.

"Two friends of yours came and asked for you this afternoon," said Loke, who was following behind. "They said to tell you to meet them tomorrow or the day after at the klab or klob or whatever you call it—"

"Club."

"That's it! The club!"

"If they come back, tell them I'm busy and can't go."

"All right," said Loke.

There was a pleasant smell of cooking in the hall. Mark-Alem paused for a moment outside the drawing room, without quite knowing why. Finally he opened the door and went in. The great room, with its floor covered with rugs, was full of the familiar scents of a wood fire. Two of his three maternal uncles were there—the eldest, who had his wife with him, and the youngest—also two of his cousins, both deputy ministers. Mark-Alem greeted them all in turn.

"You look tired," said the older of the two uncles.

Mark-Alem shrugged, as if to say: "I can't help it—it's the work. . . ." He guessed at once that they'd come to talk about him and his new job. He looked at his mother, who was sitting with her legs drawn up beside her near one of the big copper braziers. She gave him a faint smile, and at once his anxiety vanished. He sat down at one end of a divan and hoped he'd soon stop being the center of attention. He didn't have to wait very long.

The older uncle took up a story he'd apparently been telling before Mark-Alem came in. He was the governor of one of the remotest regions in the Empire, and every time he came to the capital on business he brought back a lot of extremely rough stories which always seemed exactly the same to Mark-Alem as those he'd told the last time. His wife, a sickly-looking woman with a sullen expression, listened intently to all her husband said, occasionally glancing at the others as if to say, "You see the sort of place we have to live in!" She never stopped complaining about the climate there and about how hard her husband had to work; beneath all this you could detect a muted but permanent resentment against her brother-in-law, the middle one of the three uncles—the Vizier, as everyone called him now. He wasn't present this evening. As foreign minister he was the highest-ranking member of the whole Quprili family, and the governor's wife bore him a secret grudge for not doing enough to get his brother recalled to the capital.

The youngest uncle listened to the eldest with an absent smile. While Mark-Alem saw the older of the two men as a bronze figure corroded by the coarseness and fanaticism of provincial life, his liking for the younger increased daily. He had fair hair, and with his light-colored eyes, reddish mustache, and half-German, half-Albanian name, Kurt, he was regarded as the wild rose of the Quprili tribe. Unlike his brothers he had never stuck to any important job. He'd always gone in for strange occupations as brief as they were odd: At one time he'd devote himself to oceanography, at another to architecture, and lately it had been music. He was a confirmed bachelor, went riding with the Austrian consul's son, and was said to carry on a sentimental correspondence with several mysterious ladies. In short, he led a life that was as pleasant as it was frivolous, the absolute opposite of the lives led by his brothers. Mark-Alem might have thought of imitating him, but he knew he was incapable of it. Now, listening quite serenely to his uncles, he thought of the carriage that had brought them here, drawn up outside his house. Every time he saw the vehicle it filled him with a kind of fearful joy, because it had always been the bearer of news, whether good or bad.

The Palace—as among themselves all the family called the residence of the most eminent of the Quprilis—was equipped with several carriages, all identical. But for Mark-Alem they had all merged into one: *the* carriage, sometimes of good and sometimes of evil omen, with Q carved on its doors, which might convey either rainbows or thunderclouds from the main to the other family residences. On several occasions it had been suggested that the Q should be replaced by a K—in accordance with the official Ottoman spelling of their patronymic: *Köprülü*—but the family always refused, and continued to spell its name in the Albanian fashion.

"So you're working in the Tabir Sarrail?" said the elder of the two uncles, having at last finished speechifying. "You finally made up your mind?"

"We all decided together," said Mark-Alem's mother.

"You did the right thing," said the uncle. "It's an honorable position, an important job. My best wishes for your success!"

"Thank you. *Insh'Allah!*" said Mark-Alem's mother.

The two cousins now joined in the conversation. As he listened to them, Mark-Alem remembered the endless discussions the question of his job had given rise to before the Tabir was finally chosen. Any outsider hearing them would have been incredulous. How could there be such earnest arguments over a job for a Quprili, the illustrious family that had given the Empire not only five prime ministers but also countless ministers, admirals, and generals, two of whom had led campaigns in Hungary, another in Poland, while yet another had invaded Austria. Even today, despite its relative eclipse, the Quprili family was still one of the pillars of the Empire, the first to have launched the idea of its reconstruction in the form of the U.O.S. (the United Ottoman States), and the only family that had an entry to itself in the Larousse encyclopedia. It was included there under the letter K. The entry read: *KÖPRÜLÜ: great Albanian family which provided the Ottoman Empire with five Grand Viziers be-*

tween 1666 and 1710. It was on this family's door, more-
over, that the highest functionaries of the State knocked
timidly when they sought protection, advancement, or clem-
ency. . . .

But incredible as the business of Mark-Alem's job might
seem to others, in the eyes of those who knew something
about the family's history, it was a different matter. For
nearly four hundred years the Quprilis had seemed fated
equally to glory and to misfortune. If its chronicles included
great dignitaries, secretaries of state, governors, and prime
ministers, they also told how just as many members of the
family had been imprisoned or decapitated or had simply
vanished. "We Quprilis," as Kurt, the youngest of the three
uncles, would say half jestingly, "we're like people living at
the foot of Vesuvius. Just as they are covered with ashes when
the volcano erupts, so are we every so often struck down
by the Sovereign in whose shadow we live. And just as the
others resume their ordinary lives afterward, cultivating
the soil that is as fertile as it is dangerous, so we, despite the
blows the Sovereign rains on us, go on living in his shade and
serving him faithfully."

Ever since he was a child, Mark-Alem could remember the
servants coming and going in the house in the middle of the
night; the whispering in the corridors; terrified aunts knocking at the gate. He remembered whole days full of bad news
and waiting and anxiety, until calm was restored and people
wept placidly over the doomed prisoner in his cell, and life
resumed its former course, awaiting a new spell of grandeur
or fresh misfortune. For as they said in the Quprili family,
either their men were appointed to highest office or else they
fell into disgrace. No half measures for them.

"It's a good thing you at least aren't a Quprili by name,"
Mark-Alem's mother would say sometimes, not really con-

vinced even herself. He was her only child, and after her husband's death her only care had been to protect her son from the less desirable aspect of the Quprili destiny. This preoccupation had made her more intelligent, more authoritative, and, astonishingly, more beautiful. For a long time, deep down inside, she had made up her mind that Mark-Alem should not go into government service. But by the time he'd grown up and finished his studies, this decision seemed untenable. The Quprili family brooked no idlers, and he had to be found a job somehow—one that offered the most possibilities for making a career and the least for ending up in prison.

In lengthy family discussions they had considered diplomacy, the army, the court, banking and administration. They'd weighed the pros and cons of all of them, the chances of promotion and dismissal. One possibility would be ruled out because it seemed unsuitable or dangerous; another would be rejected for similar reasons; a third might appear different at first, and quite safe, but on closer examination it would turn out to be more risky than its predecessors. So the discussion would go back to the first suggestion, previously set aside with "Oh, God, anything but that!"—and so on and so forth, until Mark-Alem's mother, exasperated by all the chopping and changing, finally said: "Let him do what he likes—you can't escape what is written!"

At that point, just as they were going to let Mark-Alem choose for himself, his second uncle, the Vizier, who so far had not taken part in the discussion, finally gave his opinion. At first blush what he suggested seemed so preposterous that it provoked smiles, but it wasn't long before the smiles faded and every face took on an expression of stupefaction. The Palace of Dreams? How? Why? Then the idea gradually came to seem quite natural. After all, why not? What was wrong with working in the Tabir Sarrail? Not only was there nothing wrong, but it was in fact a much better job than most of the others, which were strewn with pitfalls. But was there really no danger in this case? Yes, of course there were risks, but they were of dream dangers in a world of dreams—the very world the Ancients used to wish to be transported to when they were in trouble and cried, "Oh, God, let it be only a dream!"

So that was how it came about. Little by little the minister's idea took root in the mind of Mark-Alem's mother. How was it they hadn't thought of it before? she wondered. The Tabir now seemed the only institution capable of ensuring her son's happiness. It offered unlimited opportunities for making a career, but in her eyes its main advantage lay in its vagueness and impenetrability. Reality split in two there and led swiftly to unreality; and the resulting mistiness seemed to her likely to offer her son the best possible refuge when storms broke.

The others came around to her opinion. What's more, they thought, if the Vizier had initiated the idea there must be something in it. The Tabir Sarrail had recently been playing a more important role in matters of State. The Quprilis, naturally inclined to regard old and traditional institutions with some irony, had rather underestimated the Palace of Dreams. It was said that some years earlier they had managed to curtail its power, though not to have it closed down altogether. But at present the Sovereign had restored it in all its former authority.

Mark-Alem had learned all this gradually, in the course of the long family debates about the kind of employment that would be best for him. Naturally, the fact that the Quprilis somewhat underestimated the Tabir didn't mean they didn't have agents there. If they'd been so heedless as to ignore the place completely, they'd long ago have ceased to be what they were. Nevertheless, absorbed as they appeared to be in other

state mechanisms, and confident that they would again suc-
ceed in neutralizing what they jokingly called among themselves "that woolly institution," they had ceased to pay it
much attention. Now, however, they seemed to be trying to
make up for this negligence.

Although they had their own representatives in the
Tabir—and scores of them, at that—you couldn't, said the
Vizier to his sister, rely on them as surely as you could on
people of noble blood. He was obviously nervous, and she got
the impression that he was more anxious about this matter
than he cared to admit. He must have more in mind than he'd
revealed to her.

This particular interview had taken place two days before
Mark-Alem presented himself at the Tabir Sarrail. But ever
since the Vizier first made the suggestion, Mark-Alem's name
had always been linked with that of the Palace of Dreams.
They were still being joined together now, and that was why
the present conversation was getting on his nerves. He hoped
they'd change the subject when they sat down to dinner.
Luckily they did so even before. The theme was still the Tabir
Sarrail, but not in relation to him. Mark-Alem began to take
more interest.

"Anyhow, it's true to say the Tabir Sarrail has now recov-
ered all its old authority," said the elder of the uncles.

"For my part," observed Kurt, "even though I am a
Quprili, I've never thought it could easily be undermined. It's
not only one of the oldest State institutions—in my opinion
it's also, despite its charming name, one of the most formidable."

"It's not the only one that's formidable," objected one of
the cousins.

Kurt smiled.

"Yes, but in the other ones the terror's obvious. The fear

they inspire can be seen for miles, like a cloud of black smoke. But with the Tabir Sarrail it's quite different.''

"And why, in your opinion, is the Palace of Dreams so formidable?'' asked Mark-Alem's mother.

"It isn't so in the way you may suppose,'' said Kurt, with a covert glance at his nephew. "I was thinking of something else. If you ask me, of all the mechanisms of State, the Palace of Dreams is the most remote from human will. Do you see what I mean? It's the most impersonal, the blindest, the most deadly, and so the most autocratic.''

"Even so, I reckon it too can be kept more or less under control,'' said the other cousin.

He was bald, with dim eyes that reflected his intelligence in a very peculiar way; they seemed simultaneously to reveal and to be consumed by it.

"In my opinion,'' Kurt went on, "it's the only organization in the State where the darker side of its subjects' consciousness enters into direct contact with the State itself.''

He looked around at everyone present, as if to assess the effect of his words.

"The masses don't rule, of course,'' he continued, "but they do possess a mechanism through which they influence all the State's affairs, including its crimes. And that mechanism is the Tabir Sarrail.''

"Do you mean to say,'' asked the cousin, "that the masses are to a certain extent responsible for everything that happens, and so should to a certain extent feel guilty about it?''

"Yes,'' said Kurt. Then, more firmly: "In a way, yes.''

The other smiled, but as his eyes were half closed you could see only a bit of his smile, like a shaft of light from under a door.

"All the same,'' he said, "I think it's the most absurd institution in the whole Empire.''

"In a logical world it would be absurd," said Kurt. "But in the world as it is it's quite normal!"

The cousin laughed heartily, but gradually stifled his mirth when he saw the governor's face darken.

"Yet it's rumored everywhere that things are more complicated than that," said the other cousin. "Nothing is ever as clear as it seems. For example, who can say nowadays what the Oracle of Delphi was really like? All its records have been lost—or rather destroyed. And it wasn't as easy as all that to get Mark-Alem taken on. . . ."

Mark-Alem's mother was listening attentively to all this, trying to catch every word.

"I think you'd better change the subject," said the governor.

It wasn't as easy as all that to get me taken on. . . . Mark-Alem thought to himself. And gradually there came back to him scenes from his first morning at the Tabir, when he'd been so lost and bewildered, together with glimpses of the tedious hours he'd spent today, working in Selection. I suppose he thinks I shot straight to the top of the tree! he laughed bitterly to himself.

"Come, let's talk about something else!" said the elder of the two uncles again.

At this point Loke came and announced that dinner was served, and everyone got up and went into the dining room.

At table the governor's wife started talking about the customs in her husband's province, but Kurt, none too politely, interrupted her.

"I've invited some rhapsodists to come here from Albania," he said.

"What!" cried two or three voices.

They obviously meant "Where on earth did you get that idea? What bee have you got in your bonnet now?"

"I was talking to the Austrian ambassador yesterday," Kurt continued, "and do you know what he said? He said, 'You Quprilis are the only great family left in Europe, probably in the world, who are the subject of an epic.'"

"Ah," said the elder of the uncles, "now I see!"

"According to him the epic devoted to us is in the same class as the *Nibelungenlied,* and he said, 'If a hundredth of what is sung about you in the Balkans were still sung today about a French or German family, they'd shout it from the housetops as their highest claim to fame. Whereas you Quprilis scarcely deign to notice it.' That's what he said."

"I see," repeated the other uncle. "But there's one thing I don't understand. You mentioned Albanian rhapsodists, didn't you? If you're talking about the epic we all know, what have Albanian rhapsodists got to do with it?"

Kurt Quprili looked him straight in the eye but didn't answer. Debate about the family epic was as ancient as the priceless antique vases, the gifts of various sovereigns, that were piously handed down from one generation of Quprilis to the next. Mark-Alem had heard his relations talking about the epic since his earliest childhood. At first he'd imagined the *epos,* as they called it, as a long thin animal, midway between a hydra and a snake, which lived far away in some snowy mountains, and which, like a beast of fable, carried within its body the fate of the family. But as he grew older he gradually realized what the epic really was, though still in a confused sort of way. He couldn't quite see how it was that the Quprilis lived and lorded it in the imperial capital, while people recited an epic about them in a faraway province called Bosnia in the middle of the Balkans. Why in Bosnia and not in Albania, where the Quprilis originally came from? And above all, why was it sung not in Albanian but in Serbian? Once a year, during the month of Ramadan, some rhapsodists

would come from Bosnia. They would stay with the Quprilis
for several days, reciting their long epics to their own plain-
tive musical accompaniment. It was a custom that had lasted
for hundreds of years, and recent generations of the Quprilis
hadn't dared to drop or even modify it. They would gather
in the great guest hall and listen to the dronings of the Slav
bards, not understanding a single word except *Tchuprili,* the
visitors' pronunciation of the family name. Then the rhapsodists would receive their usual reward and go home again,
leaving behind them an atmosphere of emptiness and unsolved
mystery, in which for several days their erstwhile hosts would
heave vague sighs, like those provoked by a sudden change in
the weather.

Rumor had it, however, that the Sovereign was jealous of
the Quprilis because of the epic. Dozens of diwans and poems
had been written in his honor by the official poets, but
nowhere had anyone composed an *epos* about him like the
one the Quprilis had inspired. It was even said that this
jealousy was one reason for the thunderbolts the Sovereign
regularly unleashed upon the Quprilis.

"Why don't we just give the epic to the Sultan and avert
such troubles once and for all?" little Mark-Alem had suggested one day after hearing the grown-ups repining.

"Hush!" said his mother. "An epic isn't something you
can present to someone else. It's like a wedding ring or the
family jewels—something you can't give away even if you
want to."

"He said it was in the same class as the *Nibelungenlied,*"
repeated Kurt pensively. "And for days I've been pondering
the question we've all asked so often: Why have the Slavs
composed an epic in our honor, while our compatriots the
Albanians don't mention us in *their* epic?"

"Nothing simpler," said one of the cousins. "They don't

say anything about us because they expected something of us and they were disappointed."

"So you think they ignore us out of resentment?"

"If you like."

"I can understand it quite easily," said the other cousin. "It's an ancient misunderstanding between our family and the Albanians. They can't get used to our imperial dimension, or rather they don't think it's of any consequence. They care little for what the Quprilis have done and continue to do for the Empire as a whole. All that matters to them is what we've done for the small part of the Empire that is Albania. They've always expected us to do something specially for them."

He threw out his arms as if to say, "So there you have it!"

"Some people think Albania is doomed; others think it was born under a lucky star. I think the question's more complicated than that. Albania is rather like our family—it has experienced both favor and severity at the Sultan's hands."

"And which of the two has counted most with them?" asked Kurt.

"Hard to say," answered the cousin. "I remember what a Jew said to me one day: 'When the Turks rushed at you brandishing spears and sabers, you Albanians thought they'd come to conquer you, but in fact they were bringing you a whole Empire as a present!' "

Kurt laughed.

The cousin's dim eyes seemed to emit a last spark.

"But like all madmen's gifts," said the other cousin, "it brought with it violence and bloodshed."

Kurt laughed again, more loudly this time.

"Why do you laugh?" asked his brother, the governor. "The Jew was right. The Turks have shared power with us—you know that as well as I do."

"Of course," said Kurt. "Those five prime ministers prove it."

"That was only the beginning," said the governor. "After them there were hundreds of senior officials."

"That wasn't what I was laughing at," said Kurt.

"You're a spoiled brat," muttered the other.

A glint came into Kurt's eye.

"The Turks," went on the cousin, trying to attract attention again, "gave us Albanians what we lacked: the wide open spaces."

"And wide open complications too," said Kurt. "It's bad enough when an individual life gets caught up in the mechanisms of power—when a whole nation is drawn in it's a million times worse!"

"What do you mean?"

"Weren't you just saying the Turks shared power with us? Sharing power doesn't just mean dividing up the carpets and the gold braid. That comes afterward. Above all, sharing power means sharing crimes!"

"Kurt, it's not right to talk like that!"

"Anyhow, it's the Turks who helped us to reach our true stature," said the cousin. "And we just cursed them for it."

"Not us—them!" said the governor.

"Sorry—yes . . . Them. The Albanians back home in Albania."

A tense silence followed. Loke brought in trays of cakes.

"One day they'll win real independence, but then they'll lose all those other possibilities," continued the cousin. "They'll lose the vast space in which they could fly like the wind, and be shut up in their own small territory. Their wings will be clipped, and they'll flap clumsily from one mountain to another until they're exhausted. Then they'll ask themselves, 'What did we gain by it?' And they'll start looking for what they've lost. But will they ever find it?"

The governor's wife heaved a deep sigh. No one had touched the cakes.

"Anyhow," said Kurt, "for the moment they don't say anything about us."

"One day they'll understand us," said the governor.

"We ought to listen to them too."

"But you just said they don't say anything."

"Then we should listen to their silence," said Kurt.

The governor guffawed.

"Still the same old eccentric!" he laughed. "As I said, life in the capital has spoiled you. It would do you good to spend a year working for the government in some distant province."

"God forbid!" breathed Mark-Alem's mother.

The governor's laughter had relieved the tension, and forks were stretched out to spear the cakes.

"I invited the Albanian rhapsodists to come because I wanted to hear the Albanian epic," said Kurt. "The Austrian ambassador has read parts of it, and he thinks Albanian epics are much finer than the Bosnian ones."

"Does he indeed?"

"Yes," said Kurt. He blinked as if blinded by sunlight on snow. "They talk about hunts through the mountains; single combats; the abduction of women and girls; wedding processions to marriages full of danger; *khroushks** rooted to the spot with fear lest they've made some mistake; horses drunk on wine; knights who've been treacherously blinded riding on blinded steeds through mountains holding their breath; owls foretelling woe; knockings at the gates of strange manor houses at night; a macabre challenge to a duel, issued to a

*Members of the procession escorting a bride.

dead man by a live one lurking around his grave with a pack of two hundred hounds; the moans of the dead man unable to rise from his grave to fight his enemy; men and gods quarreling, fighting, intermarrying; shrieks, battles, horrible curses; and over all, a cold sun that sheds light but never warms.''

Mark-Alem listened as if bewitched. He was filled with a strange homesickness for the distant winter snow on which he had never trod.

"That's what it's like, the Albanian epic from which we are absent," said Kurt.

"If it's anything like what you describe, no wonder we're not in it!" observed one of the cousins. "It sounds more like a melodramatic frenzy!"

"But we *are* in the Slav epic," said Kurt.

"Isn't that enough?" asked the cousin with dull eyes. "You said yourself we're the only family in Europe and perhaps in the world that's celebrated in a national epic. Don't you think that's sufficient? Do you want us to be celebrated by *two* nations?"

"You ask if that isn't enough for me," said Kurt. "My answer is no!"

The two cousins shook their heads indulgently. His elder brother smiled too.

"You haven't changed," he said. "Still the same eccentric."

"When the rhapsodists come," said Kurt, "I invite you all to come and hear them. Among other things they'll sing the old 'Ballad of the Bridge with Three Arches,' about the bridge from which our family name derives. . . .''

Mark-Alem was listening openmouthed.

"But they'll be singing it in the Albanian version," Kurt

went on. "I haven't said anything about it yet to the Vizier, but I don't think he'll object to our putting them up. They'll have had a long journey—not to mention the trouble of hiding their instruments. But it's worth it. . . ."

Kurt went on for some time, speaking with passion. He spoke again of the link between their family *here* and the Balkan epic *there,* and of the relations between government and art, the evanescent and the eternal, the flesh and the spirit. . . .

His elder brother's face had clouded over.

"Be that as it may," he said, "talk about it as much as you like between these four walls, but be careful not to do so anywhere else."

Silence fell around the table. The last clink of forks against plates only made it more tense.

To lighten the atmosphere the governor turned to Mark-Alem and said in a sprightly tone:

"We haven't heard anything from you lately, nephew! You seem to be up to your neck in the world of dreams!"

Mark-Alem felt himself blushing again. Everyone's attention was once more concentrated on him.

"You work in Selection, don't you?" his uncle went on. "The Vizier was asking me about you yesterday. A person's real career in the Palace of Dreams, he said, begins in Interpretation—that's where the genuinely creative work is done and where people's individual talents have a chance to shine. Do you agree?"

Mark-Alem shrugged as if to say *he* hadn't chosen the section he was sent to work in. But he thought he detected a secret gleam in his uncle's eye.

And though the governor had swiftly looked down at his plate, that strange gleam hadn't escaped the notice of his own sister. It was with some uneasiness that she followed the discussion about the Tabir Sarrail, in which everyone except her son was now taking part.

Yes, everyone except Mark-Alem, though he now spent his days in the very heart of the Tabir . . . His mother's mind worked feverishly. Had she spent all that time watching over her son only to throw him in the end into a cage of wild beasts? A place that, despite the honor of his appointment, was really only the blind, cruel, even fatal mechanism they'd all been describing?

Out of the corner of her eye she looked at his emaciated features. How was her Mark-Alem going to find his way in that chaos of dreams, those misty fragments of sleep, those nightmares from the brink of death? How had she ever come to let him enter such an inferno?

All around him the conversation about the Tabir Sarrail continued, but he felt too weary to listen. Kurt and one of the cousins were discussing whether the revival of the Palace's influence was related to the present crisis in the Ottoman Superstate or merely the result of chance. Meanwhile the governor kept saying: "Come, come—let's talk about something else. . . ."

Finally the visitors rose to go and have coffee in the drawing room. They didn't go home till quite late, around midnight. Mark-Alem went slowly up to his room on the second floor. He didn't feel at all like sleeping, but that didn't bother him unduly. He'd been told newcomers to the Tabir usually suffered from insomnia for the first couple of weeks. After that they were all right again.

He stretched out on the bed and lay there for some time with his eyes open. He felt quite calm. It was a painless kind of insomnia, cold and smooth. And it wasn't the only thing about him that had changed. His whole being seemed to have undergone a transformation. The great clock at the corner of the street struck two. He told himself that at about three, or half past three at the latest, he would eventually fall asleep. But even if he did, from which file would he choose his dreams tonight?

That was his last thought before he dropped off.

INTERPRETATION ...

iii.

Much sooner than he expected, even before there was any sign of spring—and he'd thought he'd spend spring at least in Selection, and possibly even summer as well—Mark-Alem was transferred to Interpretation.

One day, before the bell rang for the break, he was told the Director-General wanted to see him. "What about?" he asked the messenger—though, thinking he saw a sardonic smile on the man's face, he immediately regretted it. Clearly you didn't ask that kind of question in the Tabir Sarrail.

As he went along the corridor he was assailed by all sorts of doubts and surmises. Could he have made some mistake in his work? Could someone have appeared from the depths of the Empire and come knocking at every door, going from office to office and vizier to vizier, claiming that his valuable dream had been thrown in the wastepaper basket? Mark-Alem tried to remember the dreams he'd rejected recently, but couldn't recall any of them. Perhaps that wasn't it, though. Perhaps he'd been summoned because of something else. It was nearly always like that. When you were sent for, it was almost invariably for some reason you could never have dreamed of. Was it something to do with breaking the secrecy rule? But he hadn't seen any of his friends since he'd started working here. As he asked his way through the corridors he felt more and more strongly that he'd been in this part of the Palace before. He thought for a while this might be because all the corridors were identical, but when he finally found himself in the room with the brazier, where the square-faced man sat with his eyes glued to the door, he realized it had been the Director-General's office he had knocked at on his very first day in the Tabir Sarrail. He'd been so absorbed in his work since then that he'd forgotten it even existed, and even now he had no idea what the square-faced man's job was in the Palace of Dreams. Was he one of the many assistant directors, or the Director-General himself?

Mark-Alem stood in front of him, almost petrified with apprehension, and waited for the other to speak. But the official continued to contemplate the door, at about the height of the doorknob. Although he was by now familiar with this mannerism, Mark-Alem did wonder for a moment whether the man was waiting for someone else to arrive before he

explained why he'd sent for him. But finally the man did tear
his eyes away from the door.

"Mark-Alem . . ." he said in a very low voice.

Mark-Alem broke out in a cold sweat. He didn't know
what attitude to take. Should he say, "At your service," or
use some other polite formula? Or just stand and wait for the
ghastly news to be revealed to him? He was now convinced
he could only have been summoned about something disagreeable.

"Mark-Alem . . ." reiterated the other. "As I told you on
your first day here, you suit us."

My God! thought Mark-Alem. That strange phrase . . . I
never thought I'd hear it again. . . .

"You suit us," the senior official went on, "and that's why
from today you're being transferred to Interpretation."

Mark-Alem felt a buzzing in his ears. His eyes shifted
involuntarily toward the brazier standing in the middle of the
room. The embers were almost buried in ash, and seemed to
be wearing a sardonic smile—the kind that appears on some
people's faces accompanied by half-closed eyes. It was these
embers that had consumed Mark-Alem's letter of recommendation on the memorable day of his arrival. They now seemed
to be assuming an air of indifference.

"You're quite right not to show any satisfaction," said the
voice.

And Mark-Alem wondered, How *am* I reacting?

As a matter of fact he didn't feel any pleasure, though he
knew he ought to be grateful, the more so as he'd been half
dead with anxiety up till a few moments ago. He opened his
mouth to say something, but the official's voice interrupted.

"I understand. If you don't express any pleasure it's because you're so conscious of the responsibility attaching to
your new duties. Interpretation is rightly known as the nerve

center of the Tabir. The salaries there are higher, but the work is more difficult—you'll often have to do overtime—and above all the responsibility is greater. Nevertheless, you must realize you're being done a favor. Don't forget that the road to the heights in the Tabir Sarrail passes through Interpretation.''

For the first time he actually looked at Mark-Alem. Not at his face, but at his midriff—where the door handle would have been if he'd been a door.

The road to the heights in the Tabir passes through Interpretation, thought Mark-Alem to himself. He was about to say he might not be up to the requirements for so difficult a task as deciphering dreams when the other, as if he'd read his thoughts, got in first.

''The interpretation of dreams as practiced in the Tabir Sarrail is difficult, very difficult. It bears no resemblance to ordinary, popular interpretation—a snake a bad omen, a crown a good one, and so on. Nor has it anything in common with all the books on the subject. Interpretation in the Tabir is on a quite different and much higher level. It uses another kind of logic, other symbols and combinations of symbols.''

''That puts it even further beyond me,'' Mark-Alem was tempted to say. He'd been frightened enough at the thought of dealing with traditional symbols—it would be far worse if he had to cope with new ones! He finally opened his mouth to speak, but was again interrupted.

''You may be wondering how you'll ever manage to learn the techniques. Don't worry, my boy—you *will* learn, and quite quickly too. Most people start off like you, hesitating and unsure of themselves, but many of them have gone on to become the pride and joy of the department. You'll master the job in a couple of weeks, three at the most. And then—'' here he beckoned, and Mark-Alem took a step forward—

"that'll be it. To try to learn more would be counterproductive; it could encourage you to work too mechanically. For the work in Interpretation is above all creative. It mustn't carry the analysis of images and symbols too far. The main thing, as in algebra, is to arrive at certain principles. And even they mustn't be applied too rigidly, or else the true point of the work could be missed. The higher form of interpretation begins where routine ends. What you must concentrate on are the permutations and combinations of symbols. One last tip: All the work that's done in the Tabir is highly secret, but Interpretation is top top secret. Don't forget it. And now off you go and start your new job. You're expected there. Good luck!"

The official's eyes were already riveted on the door again as Mark-Alem, overwhelmed, went out of it. He wandered the corridors in a state of bewilderment until at last he pulled himself together and remembered he was looking for Interpretation. The corridors were all completely deserted. The morning break must have gone by while he was with the official; he could tell from the characteristic silence that always descended after the interval. He walked on for a long time, hoping to meet someone from whom he could ask the way. But there was no one in sight. Sometimes he would think he heard footsteps ahead of him, around a bend in the corridor, but as soon as he got there the sounds would seem to recede in another direction, perhaps on the floor above, perhaps on that below. What if I roam about like this the whole morning, he thought. They'll say I turned up late on my very first day. He got more and more worried. He should have asked the way from the assistant director, or the Director-General, or whoever the hell he was!

On he went. The passages seemed alternately familiar and strange. He couldn't hear so much as a door being opened.

He went up a broad staircase to the floor above, then came back again and soon found himself on the floor below. Everywhere he met with the same silence, the same emptiness. He felt it wouldn't be long before he started screaming. He must now be in one of the remoter wings of the building; the pillars supporting the ceiling looked slightly shorter. Suddenly, just as he was going to turn back, he thought he saw a figure at the next bend in the corridor. He went toward it. A man was stationed in front of a door, and before Mark-Alem could come near he signed to him to stop. Mark-Alem halted.

"What do you want?" said the stranger. "No one's allowed here."

"I'm looking for Interpretation. I've been going round in circles for an hour."

The man examined him suspiciously.

"You work in Interpretation and you don't even know how to get there?"

"I've just been transferred there, but I don't know where it is."

The other went on scrutinizing him.

"Turn back the way you came," he finally brought out, "and follow the corridor till you get to the main stairs. Then go up to the next floor and take the passage on the right from the landing. You'll find Interpretation straight in front of you at the end."

"Thank you," said Mark-Alem, turning round.

As he went along he kept repeating, so as not to forget: along the corridor to the main stairs, next floor, passage on the right . . .

Who can he be, the man who just helped me? he wondered. He looked like a sentry, but what on earth is there to guard in this world of the deaf and dumb? This palace certainly is full of mysteries.

As he approached the stairs he thought he could see a wan light coming down from the glass roof over the stairwell. He breathed a sigh of relief.

He'd been working in Interpretation for nearly three weeks. For the first fortnight he'd been attached to some of the older hands, to be initiated into the secrets of the department. Then one day his boss came and said, "You've learned enough now. From tomorrow on you'll be given a file of your own."

"So soon?" said Mark-Alem. "Am I really up to working all on my own?"

The boss smiled.

"Don't worry. That's how everyone feels at first. But the room supervisor's over there—if you have any doubts about anything you can consult him."

Mark-Alem had been working on his file for four days, and his brain had never felt so confused. His work in Selection had been harassing enough, but compared with this it was child's play. He'd never have dreamed the work in Interpretation could be so diabolical.

He'd been given a file that was supposed to be an easy one—it was marked *Law and Order: Corruption*. But he sometimes thought: My God, if I lose my head with a file like this, what shall I do when I get one that deals with conspiracies against the State?

The file was stuffed with dreams. Mark-Alem had read about sixty of them, and had set aside a score or so that at first sight he thought he might be able to decipher. But when he went back to them, instead of looking the easiest, they looked the most difficult. So then he selected a few others, but after an hour or two they also had come to seem utterly confused and impenetrable.

It's quite impossible! he kept telling himself. I shall go mad! Four whole days and I haven't managed to unscramble one dream.

Every time some elements of a dream began to make sense he would be struck by a doubt, and what had seemed intelligible a moment before became inexplicable again.

The whole thing is pure folly! he thought, burying his face in his hands.

He was obsessed with the fear of making a mistake. Sometimes he was convinced it was impossible to do anything else, and that if anyone got anything right it was purely by chance.

Sometimes he would get frantic with worry. He still hadn't submitted one decoded dream to his superiors. They probably thought him either incompetent or else excessively timid. How did the others manage? He could see them filling whole pages with their comments. How could they look so calm?

As a matter of fact, every decoder was allowed to leave aside some dreams that he couldn't unravel himself, and these were sent to the decoders par excellence, the real masters of Interpretation; but of course not everything could be sent to them.

Mark-Alem rubbed at his temples to disperse the blood that seemed to have accumulated there. His head was a flurry of symbols: Hermes's staff, smoke, the limping bride, snow . . . They all whirled around in a wild saraband, displacing every perception of the ordinary world. To hell with it, thought Mark-Alem, taking up pen and paper, I'll give this dream the first explanation that comes into my head, and hope for the best!

It had been dreamed by a pupil at a religious school in the capital. In it two men had found a fallen rainbow. With some difficulty they raised it up and dusted it off, and one of the men repainted it; but the rainbow absolutely refused to come to life again. So the men dropped it and ran away.

Hmmm, thought Mark-Alem, fiddling with his pen. His resolution had already evaporated. But he made himself go on. Without thinking, or rather, rapidly abandoning his first explanation of the dream, he wrote underneath it: "Warning of . . ." Warning of . . .

"God, what can this nightmare possibly mean?" he almost cried out. "It's enough to drive you crazy!" He crossed out what he'd written, and tossed the sheet of paper angrily onto the heap with the other uninterpretable dreams. No, he'd sooner be sacked straightaway than have to be bothered with such drivel! He propped his head in his hands and sat with his eyes half shut.

After a while he heard the reedy voice of the room supervisor:

"What's the matter, Mark-Alem? Have you got a headache?"

"Yes, a slight one."

"Never mind—it happens to everyone at first. Do you need anything?"

"No, thanks. But I'll ask you to explain some things to me in a little while."

"Oh? Good. I've been waiting for you to do that for the past few days."

"I didn't want to bother you for nothing."

"Oh, you don't have to worry about that. That's what I'm here for."

"I'll have something for you in an hour or so," said Mark-Alem. "Only . . ."

"Only what?"

"Only I'm not quite sure . . . My explanations may be quite wrong, or may not make any sense at all."

The supervisor smiled.

"I'll be waiting for you," he said, and moved away.

Now I've got no escape, thought Mark-Alem. Whether I like it or not I'll have to get on with it the same as all the others. Well, to hell with it—here goes! And he looked for the piece of paper recording a dream in which a group of men in black crossed a ditch and disappeared into a snow-covered plain. Suddenly the meaning of the dream seemed quite clear to him: A group of officials who'd committed some fraud against the State had overcome the obstacles ranged against them and reached the safety of the white plain; this meant the fall of the government.

Mark-Alem swiftly wrote down this explanation, but hadn't completed the last few words before he thought to himself: But this is practically tantamount to a plot against the State!

He reread his interpretation and was confirmed in the thought that the dream really did relate to some kind of conspiracy. But the file he'd been given was the one concerning law and order and corruption! He was in such despair the pen fell from his nerveless hand. For once he thought he'd managed to produce something, and it turned out to be no good again! But wait a minute, he reflected. Perhaps it isn't quite as bad as that. After all, there's not all that much difference between corruption and a conspiracy against the State, since officials are involved in both cases.

Then again—how stupid of him not to have thought of it before!—the classification of the files wasn't as rigid as all that, and there was no reason why the file on law and order shouldn't also contain dreams concerning important affairs of State. And hadn't the staff often been told it was considered commendable for them to search for signs of special significance in places where at first sight there seemed to be nothing out of the ordinary? Yes, he could remember being told that quite plainly. It was even said that many Master-Dreams had come from the most undistinguished of files.

Mark-Alem felt much better now. Before the impulse had time to weaken, he took up four dreams that he'd read several times already and added his own explanation of each of them. He was feeling quite pleased with himself, and getting ready to deal with a fifth dream, when for some unknown reason he looked at the first dream again, and reread the explanation he'd appended to it. He was immediately overcome with doubt. Could I be mistaken? Could the dream have another explanation? he thought. A moment later he was quite sure he'd got it wrong. Beads of cold perspiration broke out on his forehead; he sat staring at the lines he'd written such a short time ago with so much alacrity, which now seemed alien and hostile. What ought he to do?

Then he said to himself, Dash it all, who's going to attach any importance to this one dream out of all the tens of thousands that are dealt with here? And he was just about to leave it as it was when at the last moment his hand dropped away again. What if someone discovered his mistake? Especially as the dream involved State officials! Government circles might get to know of it somehow, and the worst of it was that everybody might think the accusation applied to themselves or their associates. A search would be made for the person who'd supplied the explanation of the dream, and when they found out it was him they'd say: "Well, well, a fellow called Mark-Alem, a new boy who's only just started in the Tabir Sarrail, and as soon as he starts decoding his first dream he tries to sling mud at the senior servants of the State. Better keep an eye on that snake in the grass!"

Mark-Alem hastily snatched the page up as if to prevent anyone from reading what he'd written. He absolutely must try to repair his blunder before it was too late. But how? It occurred to him that he might simply do away with the dream altogether, but then he remembered that the cover of each file indicated the number of dreams it contained. To abstract one of them would be enough to get you sent straight to prison as a common thief. Something else, something else—he must think of something else! If he hadn't been in such a hurry, if he hadn't dashed the words off so madly, he could now have given the dream a completely different explanation. It was some diabolical impulse that had made him hurl himself upon his own destruction. It was all up with him now. But not so fast, he thought, still gazing at his own writing; perhaps all is not lost yet.

His eyes flew over the words again, and concluded there was still a possible way out. When he'd reread the page for the third time, he was surprised he hadn't thought of it before. An unexpected sense of relief spread from his temples to his throat and lungs. After all, it was quite usual to make corrections. He would do his in such a way that they wouldn't call attention to themselves; they'd just look like improvements in accuracy, refinements of style. It would be enough if he merely altered one word. For the umpteenth time he reread the phrase "a group of officials who'd committed some fraud against the State." Finally, with a shaky hand, he altered it to read "a group of officials who'd prevented some fraud against the State." He checked it a couple of times. It seemed all right. You could scarcely see the alteration. And even if anyone did notice it they might put it down as the correction of a slip. He breathed a sigh of relief. The business was settled at last. . . . Mark-Alem, who'd committed a fraud against the State . . .

He looked about him in terror. What if someone had noticed what he was doing? Nonsense, he told himself. The clerk who was nearest to him, and worked at the same table, was too far away to be able to read the name of his file, let alone what he'd written. A good thing my writing's so spidery, he thought. Now, after all this agitation, he could take a bit of a rest. What a beastly job!

He cast a covert glance around the rest of the room. The clerks were working peacefully away, crouching over their files. You couldn't even hear the sound of their pens. Every so often one of them would leave his desk and slip away as quietly as possible to the door. No doubt he was going down to the Archives to consult relevant interpretations made in the past—ages ago, some of them, and by decoders eminent in their art. God! he thought, looking at those dozens of heads bent over their files.

In those files was all the sleep in the world, an ocean of terror on the vast surface of which they tried to find some tiny signs or signals. Hapless wretches that we are! thought Mark-Alem.

He made himself read some more pages, but he could feel that his brain had seized up. Even if his eyes followed the text, his mind was elsewhere. Some soldiers with their faces covered up. Thousands of shoes in a village square, with a wire fixed overhead. More snow, but this time heaped up in big chests, together with a . . . set of man's clothes! My mind's gone completely, he thought, and suddenly, with a strange, almost wistful feeling, he remembered his first dream here in this palace. Three white foxes on the minaret of the local mosque. A nice dream, that, perfectly plain and clear. Where was it now, in all this horrible sea? "Oh, well," he sighed, and picked up another page. He'd have to decode at least another two before the break. But the bell rang early, it seemed to him, and he shut up his file.

There was the usual bustle downstairs. The basement where they had coffee or *salep* was the only place where you had the opportunity to exchange a few words with people you knew, or even with people you didn't. Mark-Alem had been in Selection such a short time he'd met only a few of those who worked there, and he saw them even more rarely in the cafeteria. But even when he did see them they seemed strange and far away, as if they belonged to a distant period of his existence. He preferred to talk to strangers. He hadn't spent a single satisfactory day in Selection, and perhaps that was why he avoided his former colleagues there.

In Interpretation the days were just as tedious and dreary—apart from today, when at last he'd managed to get somewhere. Maybe that was why, instead of going down to the cafeteria in the usual bitter mood, he now felt comparatively cheerful.

"Where do you work?" he said casually to the man opposite him. He'd found a place free at a table covered with empty cups and glasses.

The other man drew himself up as if in the presence of a superior.

"In the copying office, sir," he said.

Mark-Alem knew he'd been right. You could tell straightaway that the man was new to the place, as he himself had been a month ago. After taking a sip of coffee:

"Have you been ill?" he asked, surprised at his own temerity. "You're very pale."

"No, sir," the other man answered, putting his glass of *salep* down for a moment. "But we've got a lot of work, and . . ."

"Yes, of course," Mark-Alem went on as before, not quite sure where this new nonchalance of his was coming from. "Perhaps this is the high season for dreams?"

"Yes, yes," said the other, nodding his head so energetically Mark-Alem thought his thin neck would snap if he went on much longer.

"What about you?" said the other man timidly.

"I'm in Interpretation."

The eyes of his interlocutor widened, and he smiled as if to say, "I thought as much."

"Drink up—it'll get cold!" said Mark-Alem, noticing that the other man was too impressed to pick up his glass.

"It's the first time I've met a gentleman from Interpretation," he said reverently. "What a treat!"

He took up his glass of *salep* several times, but then put it down again, unable to bring himself to raise it to his lips.

"Have you been working in the Palace long?"

"Two months, sir."

And after only two months you're all skin and bones, thought Mark-Alem. Heaven knew what he himself would look like soon. . . .

"We've had a terrible lot of work lately," said the other, finally drinking his *salep*. "We've been having to do several hours' overtime every day."

"That's obvious," said Mark-Alem.

The other smiled as if to say, "What can I do?"

"It so happens that the solitary rooms are near our offices," he went on, "so when they need copyists during an interrogation they send for us."

"Solitary rooms?" said Mark-Alem. "What are they?"

"Don't you know?" said his companion. Mark-Alem immediately regretted asking the question.

"I've never had anything to do with them," he muttered, "but of course I've heard of them."

"They're more or less adjacent to our office," said the copyist.

"Are they in the part of the Palace guarded by sentries?"

"That's right," said the other cheerfully. "The guard stands just outside the door. Have you been there, then?"

"Yes, but on other business."

"Our offices are just nearby. That's why the people who work there apply to us when they need copyists. Yes, the work is really diabolical. There's someone there at the moment that they've been questioning for forty days on end."

"What did he do?" asked Mark-Alem, yawning as he spoke so as to make the question seem more casual.

"What do you mean—what did he do? Everyone knows that," said the other, looking Mark-Alem deep in the eye. "He's a dreamer."

"A dreamer? What of it?"

"As you probably know, those are the rooms where dreamers are held whom the Tabir Sarrail has sent for to ask them for further explanations about the dreams they've sent in."

"Oh, yes, I've heard about it," said Mark-Alem. He was on the point of yawning again, but at that moment, for the first time, he noticed the light fade out of the other man's eyes.

"Perhaps I oughtn't to have mentioned it, because it's secret, like everything else here. But seeing you said you worked in Interpretation, I thought you'd know all about it."

Mark-Alem started to laugh.

"Are you sorry you spoke? Don't worry. I really do work in Interpretation, and I know much more important secrets than the one you've told me about."

"Of course, of course," said the other, pulling himself together.

"What's more," added Mark-Alem, lowering his voice,

"I'm a member of the Quprili family. So you haven't got anything to worry about. . . ."

"Goodness me," said the copyist, "I had a presentiment! . . . Aren't I lucky you were good enough to talk to me! . . ."

"And how are things with the dreamer in the solitary room?" interrupted Mark-Alem. "Is there any progress? You're a copyist, you say?"

"Yes, sir, and I've been working there lately. That's where I've just come from. How are things going with him? Well, how can I put it . . . ? So far we've filled hundreds of pages with his depositions. Of course he's completely at sea, but that's not his fault. He's only an ordinary sort of chap from a dead-and-alive province on the eastern borders. It can never have entered his mind, when he sent in his dream, that he'd wind up in the Tabir Sarrail."

"And what's so important about his dream?"

The other man shrugged.

"I don't know, myself. At first glance it seems ordinary enough, but there must be something there since they're making such a fuss about it. It seems Interpretation sent it back for further explanations. But even though they're taking all this trouble, it isn't getting any clearer—in fact, it's only getting more confused."

"I don't see what they can expect to get from the dreamer himself."

"I can't really explain. I don't understand it very well myself. They ask him for further details about a few points that seem strange or unusual. Naturally he can't supply them. It's such a long time ago since he had the dream. . . . And anyway, after being shut up here so long, he doesn't know where he is. He can't even remember the dream anymore."

"Does this sort of thing happen often?"

"I don't think so. Twice or three times a year—not more. Otherwise people would get frightened and think twice about sending in their dreams."

"Of course. And what are they going to do with him now?"

"They'll go on questioning him until . . ." The copyist threw up his hands. "I don't really know."

"All very odd," said Mark-Alem. "So you can't send your dreams to the Tabir Sarrail with impunity. One fine day you might get a letter telling you to present yourself here."

The other might have been going to answer, but at this point the bell rang for the end of the break. They said good-bye and went their separate ways.

As he made his way upstairs Mark-Alem couldn't shake off the thought of what he'd just heard. What were those solitary rooms the copyist had been talking about? At first blush it all seemed absurd and inexplicable, but there must be more to it than that. What was involved was undoubtedly some kind of imprisonment. But for what purpose? The copyist had said it was obvious the prisoner couldn't remember anything about his dream. That must be the real object of his incarceration: to *make* him forget it. That wearing interrogation night and day, that interminable report, the pretense of seeking precise details about something that by its very nature cannot be definite—all this, continued until the dream begins to disintegrate and finally disappears completely from the dreamer's memory, could only be called brainwashing, thought Mark-Alem. Or an *undream,* in the same way as *unreason* is the opposite of reason.

The more he thought about it, the more it seemed this was the only explanation. It must be a question of flushing out subversive ideas which for some reason or other the State needed to isolate, as one isolates a plague virus in order to be able to neutralize it.

Mark-Alem had reached the top of the stairs and was now going along the long corridor together with dozens of his fellow workers, who disappeared in small groups through the various doors. The closer he got to the Interpretation rooms, the more the temporary sense of self-assurance he'd had in the cafeteria faded away, as it usually does when it derives from someone else's sycophancy. In its place came the feeling of suffocation that descended on him at the thought of becoming once again an insignificant clerk in the heart of the gigantic mechanism.

As he approached he could see his desk with his file lying on top of it. Going and sitting down at it was like stationing himself on the shore of universal sleep, on the borders of some dark region that threw up jets of menacing blackness from its unknown depths. "God Almighty protect me," he sighed.

The weather had grown even more severe. Even though the big tiled stoves were filled with coal and lighted first thing in the morning, the Interpretation rooms were freezing. Sometimes Mark-Alem kept his overcoat on. He couldn't understand where such extreme cold came from.

"Can't you guess?" said someone he was having coffee with in the cafeteria one day. "It comes from the files—the same place as all our troubles come from, old boy. . . ."

Mark-Alem pretended not to hear.

"What else can you expect to issue from the realms of sleep?" the other went on. "They're like the countries of the dead. Poor wretches that we are, having to work on files like that!"

Mark-Alem walked away without answering. Afterward he thought the man might have been a provocateur. Every day he was more convinced that the Tabir Sarrail was full of strange people and secrets of every kind.

The things he'd heard, during this time, about the Tabir and everything that went on there! At first it had seemed as if the people who worked there never spoke about it, but as the days went by and he picked up an odd phrase in the cafeteria, and another in a corridor, or on the way out of the front doors, or coming from the next table, there gradually, unconsciously, began to build up in his mind a large and extraordinary mosaic. Some voices said, for example, that dreams, regarded as private and solitary visions on the part of an individual, belonged to a merely temporary phase in the history of mankind, and that one day they would lose this specificity and become just as available to everyone as other human activities. In the same way as a plant or a fruit remains under the earth for a while before appearing aboveground, so men's dreams were now buried in sleep; but it didn't follow that this would always be so. One day dreams would emerge into the light of day and take their rightful place in human thought, experience, and action. As for whether this would be a good thing or a bad, whether it would change the world for the better or the worse—God alone knew.

Others maintained that the Apocalypse itself was simply the day when dreams would be set free from the prison of sleep, that this was the form in which the Resurrection of the Dead, usually depicted in a trite and metaphysical manner, would really take place. Weren't dreams, after all, messages sent from the dead as harbingers? The immemorial appeal of the dead, their supplication, their lamentation, their pro-test—whatever you cared to call it—would one day be answered in this way.

Others shared this point of view, but provided it with a completely different explanation. When dreams emerged into the harsh climate of our universe, this argument ran, they would sicken and die. And so the living would break with the anguish of the dead, and thereby with the past as well, and while some might see this as a bad thing, others would see it as a liberation, the advent of a genuinely new world.

Mark-Alem was sick and tired of all this hairsplitting. But what he found still more trying were the long insipid days when no one said anything, nothing happened, and all he had to do was crouch over his file and pass from one sleep to another. It was like being in a fog that every so often seemed about to lift but most of the time remained as thick and gloomy as ever.

It was Friday. They must be quite excited in the Master-Dream officers' room. The Master-Dream would already have been chosen, and they'd be getting ready to send it off to the Sovereign's palace. A carriage emblazoned with the imperial arms had been waiting outside for some time, surrounded by guards. The Master-Dream was about to go, but even afterward the section would be in a commotion; the previous tension would persist, or at least people would be curious to know how the dream would be received at the Sultan's palace. They usually had some account by the following day: The Padishah had been pleased; or the Padishah hadn't said anything; or, sometimes, the Padishah was dissatisfied. But that happened only rarely; very rarely.

Anyhow, it was livelier in that section than in the others; the days had some pattern to them. The week went by more quickly, looking forward to Friday. In all the other sections there was nothing but boredom, monotony, and dullness.

And yet, thought Mark-Alem, everyone dreamed of working in Interpretation. If they only knew how long the hours seemed here! And as if that weren't enough, a permanent cloud of apprehension hung over everything. (Ever since the stoves had been lighted, it seemed to Mark-Alem that this constant anxiety gave off a smell of coal.)

He bent over his file and started to read again. By now he was comparatively familiar with the work and had less difficulty in finding meanings for the dreams. In a few days' time he would have finished off his first file. There were only a few pages left. He read a few boring dreams about such things as black stagnant water, an ailing cockerel stuck in a peat bog, and a case where one of the guests was cured of rheumatism at a dinner attended by *giaours.* * What stuff! he thought, laying down his pen. It's as if they'd saved the worst till the last. He thought of the rooms of the Master-Dream officers as someone in particularly depressing circumstances might think about a house where there was going to be a wedding. He'd never seen these rooms, and didn't even know what part of the Palace they were in. But he was sure that unlike the other offices, they must have tall windows that reached up to the ceiling, letting in a solemn light that ennobled everyone and everything.

"Ah well . . ." he sighed, taking up his pen again. He made himself work without stopping until the bell rang to announce the end of the day. There were two pages still left unexamined in his file. He might as well read them now and have done.

All around him arose the racket made by the other clerks as they left their desks and made for the door. But after a little while silence was restored, and the only people left in the room were the people who'd decided to stay on late. Mark-Alem felt oppressed by the emptiness left by the departure of

---

*Contemptuous term denoting Christians.

most of his colleagues. He'd felt the same every time he'd
worked late, but what could he do? It was regarded as good
form to do some voluntary overtime occasionally, not to
mention the fact that the staff were sometimes required to
stay on. Mark-Alem had resigned himself to sacrificing yet
another evening.

Cutting short a breath that had really been a long sigh, he
began to read the next to last page. That's funny, he thought
after scanning the first line. Where had he seen this dream
before? A plot of wasteland near a bridge with some rubbish,
and a musical instrument . . . He nearly let out an exclamation
of surprise. This was the first time he'd come across a dream
that he'd examined himself when he was in Selection. He felt
as pleased as if he'd met an old acquaintance, and looked
around for someone to tell about the coincidence. But there
weren't many people left now, and the nearest one was at
least ten yards away.

Still rather thrilled by his little discovery, he read the text
of the dream—casually at first, and then more and more
carefully. He couldn't find any particular significance in it.
But that didn't worry him. A lot of dreams didn't seem to
have any meaning at first—they were like smooth cliffs where
you couldn't get a foothold—but a tiny flash of inspiration
might reveal a clue. He'd manage to find the key to this dream
as he had with others. After all, he had a certain amount of
experience now. The wasteland covered with rubbish, the old
bridge, the strange musical instrument, and the furious bull—
these were all very significant symbols. But he couldn't make
out what it was that linked them together. And in the interpretation of a dream the relationship between the various
symbols was usually more important than the symbols themselves.

Mark-Alem arranged them in pairs: the bridge with the

bull, and the musical instrument with the patch of wasteland; then the bridge with the instrument, and the wasteland with the bull; and finally the bull with the musical instrument, and the bridge with the wasteland. The last arrangement seemed to yield a certain amount of meaning, but it wasn't very logical: a bull (unbridled brute force), stirred by some music (treachery, secrecy, propaganda), is trying to destroy the old bridge. If, instead of a bridge, it had been a column or the wall of a citadel, or some other symbol representing the State, the dream might have had a certain amount of meaning; but a bridge didn't stand for anything like that. Like fountains and roads, it was usually a symbol for something useful to man. . . . Just a minute though, thought Mark-Alem, suddenly finding himself short of breath. Wasn't the bridge connected with his family's own name? . . . Perhaps this was some sinister omen?

He reread the text and began to breathe more freely again. The bull wasn't really attacking the bridge at all. It was just rushing around the piece of wasteground.

It's a dream without any meaning, he thought. The pleasure of having come across it again was succeeded by a feeling of contempt. He remembered now that even when he'd seen it in Selection it had struck him as devoid of significance. He'd have done better to throw it in the wastepaper basket there and then! He dipped his pen in the inkwell and was about to mark the dream "Insoluble," when his hand remained poised in suspense. What if he left it and came back to it again in the morning? What if he asked the supervisor for advice? Though of course, while you were allowed to ask for advice, they didn't like you to do so too often. Mark-Alem started to get impatient. The best thing was to get on and have done with the file. He'd spent more than enough time on it already. . . .

He took up the last dream, dealt with it briskly, then went back to the one he'd left in abeyance. He was just hesitating and wondering again whether to mark it "Insoluble," file it away, and go home, when the head of Interpretation entered the room. He exchanged a few words in a low voice with the supervisor, looked around as if to count those who had stayed on, then whispered something else to the supervisor.

When he had gone:

"You and you," said the voice of the supervisor.

Mark-Alem looked around.

"And you two over there. And you too, Mark-Alem— you're all to stay on. The boss has just told me there's an urgent file that has to be worked out this evening."

No one said anything.

"While it's on its way, go down and have something in the cafeteria. We may have to stay on late."

They trailed out of the room one after the other. Out in the corridor they could hear the turning of keys and the shooting of bolts coming from various directions. The last stragglers were going home.

The cafeteria was particularly depressing at this late hour. The few remaining assistants, their faces drawn with fatigue; the tables pushed aside so that the floor could be swept—it all looked very melancholy. Mark-Alem asked for a *salep* and a roll, and went to stand at the farthest end of the counter. He didn't want to be disturbed. He drank his *salep* calmly and nibbled mechanically at his roll, and when he'd finished he went slowly out again, looking neither left nor right.

He stood as if stunned for a moment when he reached the endless corridor on the ground floor. It wasn't dark yet, but the shadows were gradually enfolding everything. The last vestiges of daylight came in through a window a long way up from the floor. There was no reason for him to hurry. He could just stroll about rather than go and shut himself up between the repulsive walls of the office before he had to. The corridor was completely deserted, and he suddenly felt quite pleased to be able to walk up and down alone in this vast empty space, with the big window at one end letting in a light that had faded to gray even before it passed through the dust on the windowpanes.

Mark-Alem, having just reached the stretch of corridor below the window, looked up at the rectangle of light as though from the bottom of an abyss. He was just about to go around the corner when suddenly, in this universe of the deaf and dumb, he thought he heard a noise. He stopped and listened. It sounded like footsteps approaching. Perhaps it's the caretakers checking that the doors are shut, he thought. He was about to go on when more sounds rooted him to the spot. This time they were nearer, and seemed to come from another passage that crossed the main corridor. Mark-Alem flattened himself against the wall and waited. My God, he exclaimed inwardly when he saw a group of people coming out of the side passage carrying on their shoulders a black coffin. They didn't notice him, and disappeared down a continuation of the passage from which they had come. It must be that dreamer from the provinces, he thought, as the sound of footsteps faded in the distance. He looked about him. He was just where he'd been the day he saw the sentry outside the solitary rooms. My God, he thought again—it *must* be him!

As he went up the stairs he was filled with ever-increasing anguish. He'd often thought of the unfortunate dreamer, but he'd never thought he'd end up like this! Sometimes he'd even looked for the copyist in the cafeteria to ask what had become of the prisoner—whether he'd been finally freed or was still there. But apparently the poor wretch hadn't been able to forget his dream completely. Or was it decreed in advance that whoever was summoned to the Tabir Sarrail must meet with a similar end? Monstrous! he thought, surprised at his own sudden indignation. You're not satisfied with all the rest that you destroy—you have to devour human beings as well!

When he got back to his desk he found a new file on it, which the supervisor had put there while he was away. He looked through it almost with hatred, and found it contained no more than five or six pages. He would have to study all of them that evening. The lamps had already been lighted in the room. It was colder than before; no one had put any coal on the stoves since noon. He started to read the description of the first dream, and after a few lines realized it took up the whole page and, which was very rare, seemed to be continued on the next.

Mark-Alem turned over the page, and saw that the description of the dream didn't end even there. Nor did it end on the next page. In short, to his amazement, the whole file was devoted to a single dream. He'd never come across such a long account. This must be a very special dream, he thought, and started to skim through it without stopping to look at the name and address of its author. He was going to have to spend the whole night struggling with this lengthy farrago, which was bound to turn out to be indecipherable. What a prospect!

And the dream did indeed prove to be a farrago. Such frenzied stuff was usually given to the most brilliant of the interpreters. It was even said that a long time ago a special file had been opened for this kind of thing both in Selection and in Interpretation. It was called the Frenzy File. But afterward, for reasons never quite satisfactorily explained (the real explanation was said to be the tendency to regard this file as the last straw), the practice was abandoned and such ramblings were allocated to the usual groups of dreams, according to their content. But still the supervisors in the various offices were careful to give such material to the most skillful members of staff. Mark-Alem didn't know how to take the fact that *he'd* been allocated a file of this kind. Was it an exaggerated mark of confidence in his abilities on the part of the bosses in Interpretation, or was it some kind of a trick?

Meanwhile, he went on studying the description of the dream more and more feverishly. It really was extraordinary. It started with a gang of scarecrows roving over a treeless plain which was reeking with plague generated by tiger corpses dating from the eleventh century. The whole of the first page was devoted to a description of the progress of these vagabonds, who apparently cursed a volcano called Kartoh, Karetoh, Kartokret, or something of the sort. (Its name crumbled as fast as its west face collapsed.) Meanwhile a fantastic star was shining over the plain. Then the delirious dreamer, who happened to be nearby, tried to sink into the ground, and while doing so came upon a fragment of light, like a diamond buried in the matrix of an ordinary day in universal time—an indissoluble, unbreakable fragment which even fire couldn't destroy. The brightness of the fragment of light emerging from the mud had dazzled the dreamer. And so, blinded, he had come to in hell.

What an idiot, thought Mark-Alem. He must certainly be out of his mind! But he went on reading. The other part of the text was a description of hell, but a different hell from the one people usually imagine, a hell inhabited not by human beings but by dead States, their bodies stretched out sprawling side by side: empires, emirates, republics, constitutional monarchies, confederations. . . . Hmmm, thought Mark-Alem. Well, well . . . Apart from everything else, the dream he'd thought so inoffensive at first sight was dangerous. He turned back the page to see the name of the bold fellow who'd sent it in, and read: *Dreamed in the second half of the night of December 18 by guest X—at the Inn of the Two Roberts (pashalik of central Albania).*

The wily fellow, he thought with some relief, he cleared out! (For a second he saw in his mind's eye a coffin covered in black material, now undoubtedly heading for the capital's main cemetery.) This one saw the danger at the last moment and skedaddled. . . . Mark-Alem settled down on his chair and went on reading. The States that were dead and gone to hell didn't suffer the punishments generally thought to be inflicted on men. What's more, an unusual feature of this particular hell was that its inmates could escape and come back to earth. Thus one fine day some States that had been dead for a long time and reduced to skeletons might slowly arise and reappear in the world. Only, like actors making up for another part in the same play, they had to make a few adjustments: They changed their names, emblems, and flags, though basically they remained exactly the same as before.

Well, well, thought Mark-Alem again. Accustomed as he'd always been from childhood to conversations about the State and about government affairs, he soon guessed the so-called dreamer's purpose. It was clear to him that apart from the earlier part of it, the dream was a fabrication. He found it strange that it had got through Selection. Or perhaps, because of its provocative aspect, it had been let through for ulterior reasons. But what were they? And why had the dream been sent to him in particular? Especially in this way, as a matter of urgency, to be dealt with after office hours. A chill ran down his spine. Meanwhile, his eyes went on scanning the text: *I saw the State of Tamburlaine being painted so as to cover up the bloodstains, for it was getting ready to revive; and farther on I saw the State of Herod, where the same process was under way. That State was said to be returning to earth for the third time, and it would go on reviving again and again indefinitely after seeming to collapse. . . .*

Mark-Alem straightened the papers with trembling fingers. The provocation was obvious. But he wasn't going to fall into the trap. He would show them what he was made of. He would pick up his pen and annotate the dream: "Invented as a provocation against the State for such and such a purpose, and involving the following insinuations." Yes, that's what he'd say! According to the person who'd sent in the dream, all modern States, including the Ottoman Empire, were merely old, bloodthirsty institutions buried by time, only to return to earth as specters.

Mark-Alem liked this way of putting it, and was just about to commit it to paper when he was suddenly assailed by doubt. Suppose someone said: "How is it you're so well informed about such things, Mark-Alem?" He put down his pen. He simply mustn't expose himself like that. He'd better rephrase his comments in a more restrained fashion. Something like: "Invented, with a suggestion of provocation, its suspect character reinforced by the fact that no name or address is supplied."

Yes, that's what he'd put. But anyhow, there was no sense in rushing things. All the clerks who'd been kept on late were still there. Mark-Alem looked round. The pallid light made the room, with its thin scattering of clerks, look even more dismal than usual. It was getting colder and colder. He shouldn't have taken off his overcoat. How much longer would they have to stay? He noticed that only two of the clerks were writing; the rest, like him, had buried their heads in their hands and were thinking. Had they been given normal dreams, or wild imaginings, like the one assigned to him?

Perhaps his was the only one like that? The wild ones were fairly rare, like sharks caught in a net among ordinary fish. Anyhow, it was possible that the other dreams *were* like his. Think of the sudden irruption of the head of the section, and so late—almost at the end of the usual working day. Something must have happened. Mark-Alem shivered again.

One of the other clerks got up at last, handed in his file to the supervisor, and went out. Mark-Alem picked up his pen, but reminded himself he still had plenty of time, and put it down again. It wouldn't take him more than a quarter of an hour to write his comment. He could still put it off for a while. His head was full of gloomy thoughts.

Half an hour later, another clerk left. Mark-Alem's feet were frozen. It occurred to him that if he sat there much longer his hands would get too cold to write, and this finally shook him out of his lethargy. He began his comment. At one point he heard another clerk get up and leave, but he didn't look up to see who it was. When he'd finished, there were three other people left in the room beside himself and the supervisor. I'll wait for one more to go, he told himself, and then I'll get up. For some strange reason he thought of the strangely named Inn of the Two Roberts, where the dream had originated or been fabricated. He tried to imagine the swarthy-faced traveler departing at the crack of dawn with a diabolical grin on his face, having left the sealed envelope in the letter box fixed to the inn door.

His musings were interrupted by the creak of a chair. Another clerk had gone. Now there were only two left besides himself, and he decided it would be best if he, as a newcomer to the section, left last or at least next to last. He waited for one of the others to go. Now I'll get up, he thought. Perhaps the supervisor was hoping the two who were left would get a move on.

Mark-Alem straightened up and shut his file. It must be very late. To judge by his drawn features, the supervisor was as exhausted as the rest. Mark-Alem went over and handed him his file.

"Good night!" he whispered.

"Good night," answered the other. "Do you know the way out? It's late, and all the doors of the Tabir are shut."

"Really?" It was the first he'd heard of it. "How do we get out then?"

"Through Reception, and then through the courtyard at the back," said the supervisor. "You won't have been there before, but you can't miss it. At this hour only the lights in the corridors leading that way are still on. All you have to do is follow them."

"Thank you."

When Mark-Alem got out in the corridor he saw that the supervisor was right; the lamps were lighted on only one side. He made off as instructed, listening to his own footsteps as he went; they sounded different in all that solitude. What if I get lost? he thought two or three times. Perhaps it would have been better if I'd left at the same time as one of the others who know the way. The farther he went the more nervous he felt. Still following the lights, he turned off the main corridor into a side passage, then came out again into another corridor so long he could scarcely see the end of it. The whole place was deserted. The faint glow of the lights faded into the distance. He went down two or three steps into another, very narrow passage with a vaulted ceiling. Here the lights were fewer and even more dim. How long is this going to last? he wondered. At one point he almost expected to see the men carrying the coffin appear around a corner, still wandering through the endless corridors of the vast building. If I keep on walking like this I'll go crazy, he thought. Perhaps if he just

stopped and waited, someone would turn up and show him
the way out. Or would it be better to go back to Interpretation and start out afresh with the other two? This last course
seemed the wisest, but here again there was a problem. What
if he couldn't find the way back? The devil alone knew if these
feeble lights would really lead him there.

Mark-Alem pressed on, his mouth dry despite his attempts
to reassure himself. After all, what did it really matter if he
did get lost? He wasn't on some vast plain or in a forest. He
was merely inside the Palace. But still the thought of getting
lost terrified him. How would he get through the night amid
all these walls, these rooms, these cellars full of dreams and
wild imaginings? He'd rather be on a frozen plain or in a
forest infested with wolves. Yes, a thousand times rather!

He hurried on faster. How long had he been walking now?
Suddenly he thought he heard a noise in the distance. Perhaps
it's only an illusion, he told himself. Then, after a little while,
the sound of voices burst out again, more clearly this time,
though he still couldn't tell what direction it came from.

Still following the row of lights, he went down another
two or three steps and found himself in another corridor,
which he deduced must be on the ground floor. The sound of
voices faded for a few moments, then returned, nearer.
Straining his ears, Mark-Alem walked on as fast as he could
for fear of losing what now seemed to him his only hope. But
the sound kept coming and going, without ever fading away
completely. At one point it seemed close by, but a moment
later it was far away again. Mark-Alem was practically running by now, his eyes fixed on the end of the corridor, where
a faint square of light came in from outside. Please, God, let
it be the back door! he prayed.

And it was. As he approached a little nearer he could see
it was a door. He took a deep breath, and his whole body

relaxed so suddenly he could scarcely stay upright. He tot-
tered a few more steps in the direction of the door, which
channeled into the corridor not only cold air but also the noise
he'd heard intermittently before.

When he reached the threshold an extraordinary sight met
his eyes. The rear courtyard of the Palace was filled with light
from lamps very different from those inside—a murky brightness dimmed by fog in some places, while in others patches
of wet glittered on the flagstones. The place was full of men,
horses, and wagons, some with their lights on, some with
them off, all rushing to and fro in nightmarish confusion. The
lurid glow of the lights, together with the whinnying of the
horses careering through the mist, produced an almost super-
natural spectacle.

Mark-Alem stood rooted to the spot, unable to believe his
eyes.

"What is it?" he asked a passerby who was carrying an
armful of brooms.

The other turned and looked at him in surprise, but noticing that Mark-Alem wore the badge of the Tabir on his
overcoat, answered amiably enough:

"It's the carriers of dreams, *aga*—can't you see?"

Was it really them? Why hadn't he thought of it? There
they were, rushing about in their leather tunics and muddy
boots. The wagons, their wheels, too, covered with mud, all
had the emblem of the Tabir at the back.

His eye lighted on a lean-to shed to the right of the
courtyard; there were lights on inside, and the carriers of
dreams were going in and out. That must be Reception,
where the staff was said to go on working all around the clock.
Mark-Alem started to walk across the slippery flagstones amid
the clamor of men and vehicles, some of which were trying
to find a place to draw up. He headed without thinking for

the Reception shed, meaning to take refuge there. But the uproar inside was even worse than that out in the courtyard. Dozens of dream-carriers stood by the long counters. Some had already completed their business at the delivery windows, while others awaited their turn. Some were drinking coffee or *salep,* some were eating rolls and delicious-smelling meatballs.

Mark-Alem found himself being jostled by the hefty shoulders of men in leather tunics who gave way casually to let him by, chewing, laughing, and uttering loud oaths.

So these were the famous dream-carriers, whom ever since he was a child he'd imagined as almost divine couriers driving back and forth along the roads of the Empire in their blue wagons. Some were bespattered with mud not only on their boots but almost all over; perhaps they'd had to right an overturned wagon or get a fallen horse to its feet. Their faces showed signs of anxiety, sleeplessness, and physical exhaustion. Their speech, like everything else about them, was as different as it could be from that of the sedentary staff of the Tabir. It was coarse, arrogant, and peppered with vulgar expressions. Mark-Alem, though completely lost in the midst of such an uproar, began to catch a phrase or two here and there. News from all over the Empire was to be heard here. The messengers told about the ups and downs of their journeys, their quarrels with the dim-witted clerks they had to deal with in the provinces, with drunken innkeepers, and with sentries at the roadblocks set up in troubled pashaliks.

A hoarse voice attracted Mark-Alem's attention. Without turning to look at its owner, he tried to make out what he was saying.

"My horses refused to go on," said the man. "They whinnied and snorted, but they wouldn't budge an inch. I was all alone on the steppe on the way out of Yenisehir, a remote

little town where I'd collected a few dreams—five in all for
a whole month, so you can tell what a dead-and-alive hole it
was. So there were my horses, stuck. No matter how I lashed
out with the whip they stood rooted to the spot, as they
usually do when there's a death in their path. I looked around.
There was nothing there but the empty steppe: no graves, not
a sign of any tomb anywhere. I was just wondering what to
do when I suddenly thought of the file of dreams I'd picked
up in Yenisehir. It struck me it might be because of them the
horses were petrified. Aren't sleep and death close neighbors?
So I opened my bag as fast as I could, took out the Yenisehir
file, then got down and went and dumped it some distance
away on the plain. When I climbed back on the wagon and
urged the horses forward, they started up straightaway. Blow
me down, I thought, so that was it! I stopped again and went
back and collected the file, but as soon as I put it back in the
cart the horses started acting up again just as before. What
could I do? I've transported thousands of dreams, but I'd
never had a thing like that happen to me before. So I decided
to go back to Yenisehir without the file, which I left out there
in the middle of the steppe.

"So then there was a row with the head of the Yenisehir
office of the Tabir. I told him, 'I can't take your dreams.
. . . Come and see for yourself—my horses refuse to move
as soon as I put your file in the wagon.' So the silly oaf yells,
'That makes five weeks that no one will take my dreams, and
now you want to leave them on my hands too! I'll complain,
I'll write to Head Office, to the Sheikh-ul-Islam himself!'
'Complain as much as you like,' I said. 'My horses won't stir
and you needn't think your five lousy dreams are going to
stop me from delivering all the rest.' You should have heard
him then! 'Oh, yes, of course,' he said. 'That's all you care
about *our* dreams. Naturally you find them crude—you pre-

fer the dreams of artists and courtiers in the capital. But in the highest circles it's been said it's *our* dreams that are the real ones, because they come from the depths of the Empire, not from dandies covered in paint and powder!' The swine kept on and on—I don't know how I kept my hands off him!

"Well, I didn't hit him, but I did give him a piece of my mind, I was so furious at being held up! I told him what I thought of him and his rotten little subprefecture inhabited by a handful of drunks and dodderers whose dreams were so rotten they even frightened the horses! I said that after this, if it was up to me, I wouldn't let Yenisehir have its dreams examined for at least another ten years! He was so angry he started to foam at the mouth worse than the horses! He said he was going to write a report to the authorities about what I'd said, but I said if he did I'd tell about how he'd insulted the Tabir. 'What!' he yelled. 'Me insult the sacred Tabir Sarrail? How dare you say such a thing!' 'Yes, you said it was the haunt of courtiers and painted dandies!' That was too much for that fool of a yokel, and he started to weep and ask for mercy. 'Have pity on me, *aga,*' he said. 'I've got a wife and children, don't do a thing like that. . . .' "

For a while the carrier's words were drowned in laughter.

"And what happened then?" someone asked.

"Then the subprefect and the imam came on the scene. Someone had told them about the row that was going on. When they heard what it was all about they scratched their heads at first and didn't know what to do. They didn't like to force me to take the file, because that would have amounted to keeping me there. For both of them were sure the horses would never leave if the file was up behind them. On the other hand, they couldn't admit that the dreams sent in by their subprefecture were so evil they prevented the couriers from going about their business. But my time was precious.

I was carrying more than a thousand dreams from other regions, and delay might be dangerous. So I told them to come with me to the part of the plain where I'd left the file, to see for themselves.

"They agreed to come; we all piled into the wagon, and I drove them to the place. The file was still there. I picked it up, got into the wagon with it, and whipped up the horses. They started to whinny and lather where they stood, as if the devil had got up behind them. Then I gave the file back to the subprefect and the iman, and the horses set off at a gallop. I did think of making off there and then, leaving the two officials standing there openmouthed with their file in their hands, but I thought that might get me into trouble, so I turned back. 'Did you see?' I said. 'Are you convinced now?' They were dumbfounded. *'Allah!'* they muttered. As they tried to think of a way out of the impasse, the head of the local section, terrified that he might be the first to suffer for having allowed such a diabolical letter to be sent to the Tabir at all, decided to get the letters out of the file one by one to identify the cause of the trouble and prevent the others from being implicated. We all approved of this idea, and duly took the dreams out of the bag. It wasn't difficult to find the culprit and remove it from the file. And then I was able to go on my way."

"That was no dream—it was pure poison!" said someone.

"And what will they do with it now?" asked another. "No wagon will be able to carry it, I suppose?"

"Let it stay where it is," said the man with the hoarse voice.

"But with that strange power it might be important. . . ."

"Let it be what it likes," said the courier. "If it's made of gold and the horses refuse to carry it, that means it's not a dream—it's the devil incarnate! Horns and all!''

"But . . .''

"There's no buts about it. If the horses won't bring it, it'll just have to be left to rot where it is, in that godforsaken hole of a Yenisehir!''

"No, that's not right,'' said an elderly courier. "I don't know how they manage things now, but if anything like that happened in my day we fell back on the foot couriers.''

"Were there really foot couriers then?''

"Of course. The horses didn't often refuse to carry dreams, but it did happen sometimes. And then they made use of foot couriers. There were *some* good things about the old days.''

"And how long would it take a foot courier to get the dream from there to here?''

"It depends on exactly how far it is, of course. But I think the journey from Yenisehir should take about a year and a half.''

There were two or three whistles of amazement.

"Don't sound so surprised,'' said the old man. "The government can catch a hare with an oxcart!''

They started to talk about something else, and Mark-Alem pressed on a bit farther. There was the same loud chatter everywhere, from the doors to the middle of the room and around the Reception windows, where the couriers handed in their files according to some order, the rules of which were not apparent. One fellow—Mark-Alem heard someone say he'd got drunk at an inn and lost his bag with the files inside—sat apart from all the rest, his eyes red as fire, drinking and grumbling at the same time.

From the courtyard came a constant hubbub of voices mingled with the sound of wheels on the flagstones. Some wagons had just arrived from distant parts; others were setting off again after making their deliveries. The neighing of the horses struck terror into Mark-Alem's very soul. And this is going to go on until dawn, he thought. Eventually he pushed his way through the crowd and set out for home.

A DAY OFF

...

iv.

He woke up two or three times with a start, afraid he was going to be late for work. His hand was just reaching out to throw off the blanket when his sleep-numbed brain suddenly remembered he had the day off. He lapsed back into uneasy slumber. It was the first time since he'd started working in the Palace of Dreams that he'd been given a rest day.

At last he opened his eyes. The daylight reaching his pillow was dimmed by the velvet curtains. He stretched for a moment, then threw off the blanket and got up. It

1 1 5

must be late. He went over to the mirror and looked at his face, which was still puffy with sleep. His head felt as heavy as lead. He'd never have believed that on this, his first day off, he'd wake up feeling more jaded than on the other mornings, when he had to hurry out into the damp, foggy streets to get to the office on time.

He washed his face and felt a bit fresher. It seemed to him that if he made an effort he might be able to remember two brief dreams he'd had in the early morning. Since he'd been working in the Tabir Sarrail he hardly ever dreamed. It was as if dreams no longer dared visit him, knowing he'd fathomed their secrets and could tell them to go and find someone else to play their tricks on.

As he went down the stairs he was greeted by the agreeable smell of roasted coffee and toasted bread. His mother and Loke had been waiting for him for some time.

"Good morning," he said.

"Good morning," they answered, looking at him fondly. "Did you sleep well? You look nice and rested."

He nodded, and sat down near the glowing brazier; the coffee things had been put on a low table close by. Now that he had to rush out every morning at the crack of dawn he'd almost forgotten this pleasant hour, when reflections from the silver, the coals, and the copper edges of the old brazier all combined with the pallid daylight to create the impression of an eternal morning steeped in affection.

He ate slowly, then had another cup of coffee with his mother. As usual, when she had finished she turned her cup upside down on the saucer and Loke came and read the grounds. This used to be the time when the family told one another their dreams of the previous night, but since Mark-Alem had started working in the Tabir Sarrail, this custom had been abandoned. This happened after a little incident that had occurred during his first week in the Palace, when one of his aunts had arrived in great excitement to tell him about a dream she'd had that night.

"How lucky we are!" she cried. "Now we've got the key to the meaning of dreams in our own home, and we don't need to go and see Gypsies and clairvoyants anymore!"

Mark-Alem had scowled and lost his temper—a rare thing for him. How dare this silly woman bring her stupid, uninteresting dreams to him? Who did she take him for?

At first the aunt was stupefied; then she went off in a huff, and her daughters had a lot of trouble calming her down.

Mark-Alem contemplated the embers, pale now under a layer of ashes.

"It's quite mild today," said his mother. "Are you going out for a walk?"

"Yes, I think so."

"There isn't any sun, but it will do you good to get some fresh air."

He nodded.

"Yes, it's a long time since I went for a walk."

He sat for a moment without speaking, his eyes fixed on the brazier; then he got up, put on his coat, kissed his mother good-bye, and went out.

Yes, it was a dull day, as his mother had said. He looked up to seek at least some traces of the sun in that empty sky. Its emptiness suddenly seemed unbearable. It was some time since Mark-Alem had seen the sky over the city at this time of day, and it struck him as amazingly insipid with its scattering of insignificant clouds and its few uninteresting birds. Since starting work at the Tabir he'd gone out very early in the morning, generally in bad weather and with his head still swimming after an unsettled night, and come home at dusk, too tired to pay attention to anything. So now he looked at the city like someone returned from a brief exile. He looked right and left, almost with astonishment. By now not only the sky struck him as washed-out and insipid, but also all the rest—the walls, the roofs, the carriages, and the trees. What's happening? he wondered. The whole world seemed to have lost all its color, as if after a long illness.

He had an icy sensation in his chest. His legs, after taking his body down the street where he lived, now led him toward the town center. The pavements on both sides of the road were overflowing with people, but they moved stiffly, with a kind of grudging precision. Just as niggardly seemed to him the movement of the traffic and the call of some wretched town crier in Islam Square, who sounded as if he were yelling out all the troubles in the world.

What had happened, then, to life, to mankind, to everything here below? There—he smiled inwardly as if at some precious secret—there, in his files, all was so different, so beautiful, so full of imagination. . . . The colors of the clouds, the trees, the snow, the bridges, the chimneys, the birds—all were so much more vivid and strong. And the movement of people and things was freer and more graceful, like stags running through the mist, defying the laws of space and time! How tedious, grasping, and confined this world seemed in comparison with the one he now served!

He went on gazing at people, carriages, and buildings in amazement. Everything was so ordinary, meager, and depressing! He'd been quite right not to go out and not to see anyone these last months. Perhaps that was why they gave the people who worked in the Palace of Dreams so little time off. He realized now that he didn't know what to do with it. There seemed no point in walking about this faded city.

Mark-Alem continued to cast a cold eye on all around him. It seemed increasingly clear that there was nothing accidental about what he was feeling. That other world, however exasperating he sometimes found it, was much more acceptable than this one. He'd never have believed he could become detached so quickly from the ordinary world—after only a few months' absence. He'd heard about former employees in the Palace of Dreams who had in a manner of speaking withdrawn from life while they were still alive, and who, whenever they found themselves among people they used to know, looked as if they had just come down from the moon. Perhaps he'd be like that himself in a few years' time, thought Mark-Alem. What if I am? Look at the nice world you'd be leaving behind you! The passersby directed sardonic smiles at the wild-looking employees of the Palace of Dreams, but they never dreamed how arid and wretched their own lives seemed to the visionaries from the Tabir.

He had now reached the terrace of the Storks Café, where he generally used to have a coffee in the days when he was . . . the word that came to mind first was "alive," but it was soon supplanted by "awake." Yes, this was where he used to drop in for a coffee when he was only an idle young man-about-town. He went in and without looking around made straight for the corner on the left and what had once been his usual seat. He liked this café. It had comfortable leather armchairs instead of the sofas still to be found in old-fashioned tearooms.

The café owner struck Mark-Alem as looking very sallow.

"Mark-Alem!" he said in surprise, coming over with the coffeepot in his hand. "Where have you been all this time? I thought at first you must be ill—I couldn't believe you'd taken your custom elsewhere."

Instead of providing an explanation, Mark-Alem only smiled. The proprietor of the café smiled too, then leaned over and whispered:

"Later on I found out what had happened. . . ." Then, seeing the other's face darken: "Will you have your coffee with a little sugar, as usual?"

"Yes, as usual," said Mark-Alem, without looking up.

He stifled a sigh as he watched the thin stream of coffee being poured into the cup. Then, when the café owner had gone away, he looked around to see if the usual customers were there. They nearly all were: the *hodja* from the neighboring mosque, with two tall men who were never heard to utter a word; Ali the acrobat, surrounded as always by a group of admirers; a squat little bald man poring as usual over some old bits of paper. These were described by the café proprietor, according to his mood, as ancient manuscripts which his learned client was arduously translating, or vestiges of an ancient lawsuit, or an abstruse and useless document found in some silly old dodderer's wormeaten trunk.

And there are the blind men, thought Mark-Alem. They were in their usual place to the right of the counter.

"They've done me an awful lot of harm!" the proprietor had confided to Mark-Alem one day. "I'd have a much better class of customer if those repulsive-looking fellows hadn't chosen to come to my café—*and* to sit in the best seats always, just to drive me really crazy! But there's nothing I can do—I have no choice. The State protects them, so I can't throw them out."

Mark-Alem had asked what he meant by "The State protects them," and the proprietor, who was expecting the question, told him a truly amazing story. The blind men who came to his café hadn't lost their sight through illness, accident, or war. If that had been the case he would have welcomed them gladly. But the cause of their blindness was different, and very difficult to comprehend. They had never suffered from any physical infirmity, and at one time could see, but their eyes, unlike other people's, had a baneful effect. And so, as Mark-Alem must know, the great Ottoman State, in order to defend itself and protect the rest of its subjects, decreed that these people were to have their eyes put out. And by way of compensation the State in its mercy awarded them each a pension for life.

"So now do you see why I can't throw them out of my café? Goodness knows who they take themselves for! They're proud of their sacrifice—probably take themselves for heroes!"

Mark-Alem hadn't known anything about this decree, and at first regarded the proprietor's story, which he probably repeated to every new client, as the creation of a deranged mind. But on looking into the matter he found the decree did exist, and that it was put into practice throughout the Empire.

Strangely enough, in spite of their black bandages, Mark-Alem didn't find them frightening anymore. *There,* in the Tabir, he had read about all kinds of terrifying looks, and he thought of those eyes now in their supreme horror, opening not out of human brows but out of the edge of the sky or the deepest heart of the mountains, and lighted sometimes by a sliver of moon like a waxen stalactite.

Neither the denunciation of people with the evil eye, which had horrified Mark-Alem when the café owner first told him about it (for anyone could write a letter accusing someone else of this offense); nor the monthly meeting of a government committee to decide which of the wretches who had been arrested really did have the evil eye and were to have it put out; nor even the cruelty itself, referred to as "in the public interest" in the traditional speech delivered to those who had just been blinded—none of these things horrified Mark-Alem now as they had done in the past. Sometimes he found himself thinking that a few years hence neither the wonders nor the horrors of this world would have any effect on him; they were, after all, pale copies of the wonders and horrors *there,* in the Tabir, which had succeeded in crossing the frontiers between this world and the other. Hell and heaven are indistinguishable there, he observed whenever he heard anyone say, "How wonderful!" or "How horrible!"

The door of the café opened, admitting some officials from the foreign consulate opposite. They still come and have coffee here, thought Mark-Alem. The acrobat's table fell silent for a moment. In the old days Mark-Alem, too, used to be rather thrilled when foreigners came into a place where he was, and used secretly to admire their European dress. But now, strangely, he found even foreigners devoid of mystery.

This was the time of the morning when the café was at its most crowded. Mark-Alem recognized some of the staff of the Vakoufs'* Bank, which was no more than a stone's throw away. Then the policeman who'd just got off traffic duty came in. The next customers were people Mark-Alem didn't know. Stifled laughter arose from the acrobat's table. Laugh away, he thought. For frivolous fellows like you, the world is a bed of roses.

But *then, suddenly,* like a dark cloud, there came back to him the dinner party two days before at the house of his powerful uncle, the Vizier. Mark-Alem hadn't seen him for nearly a year, and he'd trembled, as always, when he got home from work and saw his carriage with the Q on the doors waiting outside the house. But he'd been even more shaken to learn from his mother that the Vizier had sent the carriage to fetch him, and was waiting to see him.

*Members of the Muslim clergy.

Although the Vizier had greeted him warmly, Mark-Alem thought he looked tired and morose. His eyes were dull, as if he'd slept badly. As for his speech, it was full of pauses, and he seemed to be swallowing most of what he had to say. The worries inherent in power, thought Mark-Alem. His uncle asked him about his work, and he, at first with some awkwardness and then more and more freely, started to describe its various aspects. But the Vizier listened absently, and seemed to be thinking of something else. Soon, when Mark-Alem thought he'd just told him something interesting, he blushed to realize that not only was his uncle aware of everything that went on in the Tabir Sarrail, but he knew much more about it than all the people who worked there. The Vizier then talked to him about it, speaking in a slow voice, with many pauses, and leaving many things unexplained. Nevertheless, Mark-Alem learned much more about the Tabir Sarrail in those few minutes than in all the time he'd worked there.

They were alone—something that had never happened before—each with a cup of coffee in front of him, and Mark-Alem still didn't know why his uncle had sent for him. He was still talking in a low voice, every so often poking at the coals in the brazier, which appeared to interest him rather more than Mark-Alem did. The Vizier spoke about the Quprili family's relations with the Palace of Dreams. As his nephew might have heard, these relations had been extremely confused for some hundreds of years. It looked as if he was about to add something, perhaps about the Quprilis' feverish efforts to abolish the Palace of Dreams, but apparently he changed his mind, for he sat silent for some time, clutching the poker nervously and prodding at the coals.

"It's no secret to anyone," he said finally, "that a few years ago the Tabir Sarrail was under the influence of the banks and the owners of the copper mines, whereas more recently it has grown closer to the Sheikh-ul-Islam faction. What of it? perhaps you're wondering. Well, it's of the greatest importance! It's not for nothing that one hears it said everywhere nowadays that whoever controls the Palace of Dreams possesses the keys of the State.''

Mark-Alem had indeed heard talk on this subject, but never anything as outspoken, and certainly not from the lips of so senior a government figure. He was taken aback, and as if all that wasn't enough, the Vizier went on and asked him if he knew what became of the myriads of dreams that were examined in the Tabir Sarrail. Mark-Alem, red in the face, shrugged and said he didn't know. He was so mortified he'd have liked to sink through the floor. As a matter of fact, he had occasionally asked himself the question, and had naively supposed that once the Master-Dream had been selected, like wheat from chaff, all the useless dreams were bundled up and sent down to the Archives. But as soon as the Vizier asked the question, he told himself it was absurd to think such a mountain of dreams, after having produced the rare flower of a Master-Dream, would just be discarded. Now the Vizier explained that while the choice of a Master-Dream was the main task of the section concerned, hence its name, it was not its only function. The Master-Dream officers were also required to write notes alerting the main institutions of the State to matters of interest, as well as reports and other secret studies on such subjects as the psychoses from which the various classes and races of the Empire suffered.

Mark-Alem drank in his uncle's words. Naturally, the Vizier stressed, the Master-Dream was of prime importance, especially at times like this, and above all as regards their own family. He stared at his nephew for some time, as if to make sure he really understood that the Quprilis had never been concerned with ordinary dreams, but only, almost exclusively, with Master-Dreams.

"Do you see what I mean?" he said, his eyes veiling over, dark but glittering. "It's toward the Master-Dream that they all converge . . . all the . . ."

Again his speech grew halting.

"There are a lot of rumors going around on this subject. I shan't say whether they're true or false, but what I do want to tell you is that a Master-Dream can bring about great changes in the life of the State. . . ."

A gleam of irony appeared briefly in his eye.

"It was a Master-Dream that suggested the idea for the great massacre of the Albanian leaders at Monastir. I suppose you've heard of it? And it was a Master-Dream that caused the change of policy toward Napoleon, and the fall of Grand Vizier Yussuf. There are countless examples. . . . It's not for nothing that the power of your director, who seems quite modest and doesn't have any title, is said to rival the influence wielded by us, the most influential of the viziers. . . ."

He gave a bitter smile.

"And if he can rival us," he said slowly, "it's because he has great power at his disposal, and power not founded on facts."

Mark-Alem hung on his uncle's lips. Great power not founded on facts . . . he marveled to himself as the Vizier went on, explaining that no directive ever had or ever could come from the Tabir, nor did the Tabir need it to. It launched ideas, and its own strange mechanism immediately endowed them with a sinister power, for they were drawn, according to him, from the immemorial depths of Ottoman civilization.

"As I was saying, we Quprilis have often had dealings with Master-Dreams. . . ." he almost hissed. "They have often struck at us."

Mark-Alem remembered the nights of whispers and anxiety. In his mind's eye he saw Master-Dreams as vipers striking out with their forked tongues. The Vizier's speech was becoming more and more confused. Every so often one of his preoccupations would emerge, but he hastily covered it up again.

"You should have gone into the Tabir Sarrail before," he said, "but perhaps even now it's not too late. . . ."

More interruptions and hesitations. Mark-Alem couldn't understand what he was driving at. It was clear he didn't want to reveal what he was really thinking. But I can see his point, thought Mark-Alem. He's a statesman, and I'm only a humble clerk. Anyhow, he was leading him to understand—he was almost saying it explicitly—that he, Mark-Alem, hadn't got his job in the Tabir by chance. And he must elbow his way in, try to find out all about the way it functioned, and above all keep his eyes open so that, when the time came . . .

But so that what? And what time? He almost asked, but didn't dare. It was all so obscure. . . .

"We'll talk about it again," said the Vizier, but Mark-Alem could sense that he still couldn't bring himself to be open with him. He would keep coming back to a point in the conversation that he'd left in suspense, shed a few rays of light on it, then hastily shroud everything in darkness again.

"I expect you've heard it said that at times of crisis the power of the Tabir Sarrail tends either to decline or to increase. This is one of those times, and unfortunately the power of the Tabir is growing."

Mark-Alem didn't dare ask what the crisis was. He seemed to have heard about some project for big reforms that had greatly annoyed the clergy and the army, but he didn't really know much about it. Could the Quprilis be mixed up in that?

"This is a crucial time," said the Vizier. "The Master-Dream may strike again. . . ."

Mark-Alem concentrated, so as not to miss a word. There was a long silence.

"The question is," said the Vizier at last, "which of the two worlds dominates the other. . . ."

Off he goes again, groaned Mark-Alem to himself. Just as he seemed on the point of saying something!

"Some people," the Vizier went on, "think it's the world of anxieties and dreams—*your* world, in short—that governs this one. I myself think it's from *this* world that everything is governed. I think it's this world that chooses the dreams and anxieties and imaginings that ought to be brought to the surface, as a bucket draws water from a well. Do you see what I mean? It's this world that selects what it wants from the abyss."

The Vizier leaned closer to his nephew. His eyes now shone with a fearsome yellow light, the color of sulfur.

"They say the Master-Dream is sometimes a complete fabrication," he whispered. "Has that ever occurred to you?"

Mark-Alem went cold with fright. A fabrication? The Master-Dream? He could never have imagined a human mind daring to think such a thing, let alone say it in so many words. Still, the Vizier went on telling him the things that were said about the Master-Dream. Every now and then Mark-Alem thought, My God, it's obvious that that's what he thinks himself! . . . He still hadn't got over his amazement, and the Vizier's voice reached him as through the roar of an avalanche. So people said some Master-Dreams were forgeries; that they were fabricated in the Tabir Sarrail by the employees themselves, in accordance with the interests of powerful rival political groups or with the mood of the Sovereign; that if not entirely, they were at least partly doctored.

Mark-Alem had an almost irresistible desire to fling himself at the Vizier's feet and implore him:

"Get me out of there, Uncle! Save me!"

But he knew very well he could never do such a thing, even if he knew his work was going to lead him to the scaffold.

As he went home from the Vizier's house that night he felt anguish still nagging at him. The carriage bowled along through now unlighted streets, and sitting there in that black landau with a Q marked on each side like a fatal brand, he felt as if he were some solitary night bird flying in limbo between two worlds, and no one knew which world governed the other. . . .

He had to keep his eyes open for when the time came . . . But how would he know *when* the time came? What angel or demon would come to warn him, how would he recognize them, and with whom should he get in touch through the mists of the Tabir Sarrail?

Mark-Alem remembered this episode in the café, turning his empty cup round and round. Even now, several days later, his chest was constricted with the same apprehension. Then something made him turn toward the table occupied by the acrobat Ali's admirers, who had stopped chatting and were all goggling at him.

Mark-Alem was vexed. Apparently the café owner had told them he was working in the Tabir Sarrail. Mark-Alem knew the fellow couldn't hold his tongue, but even so . . . ! Still, he could go to the devil, he and the other busybodies with him! He probably wouldn't come to the café again more than two or three times in the next few months. Perhaps not so often; perhaps not at all.

The place gradually emptied as lunchtime approached. The foreign diplomats left; so did the bank clerks. The acrobat's admirers also got up and went, after one last astonished glance at Mark-Alem. Only the blind men didn't move. They'd stopped talking some time ago, and now sat stiff-necked, the way people do when they are angry with all and sundry. Those silent faces seemed to be saying: "Well, are affairs of State going better now that our eyes, which were supposed to harm them, have been put out? From all we hear the world is still the same as it used to be, if not worse."

At last Mark-Alem paid for his coffee, left, and began walking slowly home. After a while he was sorry he hadn't taken a cab. When he turned into his own street he heard voices whispering: "He works in the Tabir Sarrail now. . . ." He pretended not to have heard, and walked on with his head held high. The chestnut seller and the policemen at the corner greeted him with special respect. They too must have found out where he worked, and in their eyes there was a kind of wonder, as if they could scarcely believe they were still seeing him in the flesh instead of in some immaterial form.

He noticed a shape beyond the panes of a window in the house opposite. He knew that two pretty sisters lived there. He usually liked to think of them, but today even the window that generally attracted him seemed empty.

So my first visit to the world of the living is nearly over, he thought as he opened the door into the courtyard. As he moved, there was a sound like the rustle of wings, as if breezes from the beyond still clung to his body. A few nights ago, at the Vizier's house, he'd been shattered at the thought that he was risking death, but now the idea left him completely indifferent. The world was so dreary it wasn't worth tormenting oneself at the thought of losing it.

He opened the house door and went in without looking around to see what he was leaving behind him. Tomorrow . . . he thought, conjuring up the cold rooms and the files on the desks that awaited him. Tomorrow he'd be back in that strange world where time, logic, and everything else obeyed quite different laws. And he told himself that if he was ever given another day off, he wouldn't go into the town again.

THE ARCHIVES

...

V.

Directly after the morning break Mark-Alem was told the supervisor wanted to see him. Walking on tiptoe so as not to disturb anyone, he made for his superior's desk. From a few feet away he recognized, lying on top of it, the file he'd handed in to him earlier that day.

"Mark-Alem," said the supervisor, "I think it might be a good thing if for one of these dreams"—he flicked rapidly through the file—"here, this is the one. . . . I think for one of these dreams, this one, to be precise"—he plucked out the relevant page—"it might be a good idea if you went down to the Archives and looked up the interpretation previously given to this kind of thing. . . ."

For a moment Mark-Alem looked at the page, with his own explanation of the dream written at the bottom. Then he looked back at the supervisor.

"Please yourself," said the other, "but I think you should take my advice. I have a feeling this dream is important, and in such cases it's usually wise to refer to past experience."

"I don't doubt it. But . . ."

"Haven't you ever been to the Archives?" the supervisor interrupted.

Mark-Alem shook his head. The supervisor smiled.

"It's very easy," he said. "There are people there specially to help. You have only to tell them what kind of dream you want to consult them about. This is a particularly easy example: Dreams dreamed just before deadly confrontations are all kept together. I'm sure that if you glance at a few of them it'll help you to solve this one better"—tapping the sheet of paper he was holding.

"Of course," said Mark-Alem, holding his hand out for it.

"The Archives are downstairs in the basement," said the supervisor. "You're bound to meet someone in the corridors who'll tell you the way."

Mark-Alem walked steadily out of the room. Out in the corridor he took a deep breath before making up his mind which way to go. Then he remembered he had to go down to the ground floor first and start inquiring there.

He did this, and it took him nearly half an hour to get to the basement. Now what? he wondered when he found himself alone in a long vaulted passage feebly lighted by lamps attached to the walls on either side. Thinking he could hear footsteps not far off, he hurried along to join the unknown person making them; but the footsteps hurried too. He stopped; the other did the same. Then he realized that the footsteps were his own. God, he thought, it's always the same in this wretched Palace! How much would it have cost to put up a few notices showing the way to the various departments? By now he'd come to suspect that this corridor was circular. Every so often he still thought he could hear distant footsteps, but they could just as easily have been the echo of his own, or those of people on other floors. But strangely enough, he now felt quite peaceful. Whatever happened he was bound to find his way out, as he had done the other times. He was used to this kind of misadventure now. As he walked along he discovered that the circular passage was crossed by others of varying widths, but he didn't dare go along any of them for fear of getting lost. After half an hour it seemed to him he was back where he started from. I'm just going around in a circle like a horse on a threshing floor, he thought.

He stopped for a moment, breathed deeply, then resolutely advanced again. This time he turned into the first side passage he came to. He soon had reason to congratulate himself, for after he'd gone a few steps he saw a door in one wall. There was another door farther along. This must be where the confounded Archives are, he thought with relief, though he couldn't decide which of the two doors to knock at. He went on, and more doors appeared on either side. He went up to one of them, but still didn't knock. I'll try the next one, he promised himself, but once again his resolution evaporated. How could he just burst in, not even knowing where he was? Perhaps it would be better to wait until a door opened of its own accord and someone came out that he could ask. He halted, undecided. But what if someone came along, saw him standing there like a sentry, and asked him: "Hey, you—what do you think you're doing here? . . ." What a

bore, he thought, and started walking again. He felt as though
he'd done nothing else since he came to work in the Palace
but wander round the corridors without ever finding what he
was looking for. Oh, to hell with hesitations! Here goes! he
said to himself, and banged loudly on the next door he came
to. His hand sprang back at once, and if he could he would
have tried to take back his knocks, but alas, they had irrevoca-
bly thundered out inside. He waited a few seconds; no voice
was to be heard from within. He made up his mind and
knocked again, then turned the door handle. But the door
didn't open. It must be locked, he thought, and all my
dithering was pointless. He walked on a bit and knocked at
another door. This one was locked too. He tried others. They
were all shut. Where am I then? he wondered. This can't be
the Archives.

Hurrying on, he knocked no more, but with a spitefulness
he scarcely understood himself, he twisted every doorknob as
he went along. He had a wild desire to give those silent doors
a good bashing. He would certainly have set about doing so
if a door hadn't suddenly opened when he least expected it.
He'd given it such a shove he almost shot into the room. His
hand mechanically grabbed for the knob to try to close the
door again, but it was too late. The door was now wide open,
and as if that weren't enough, a pair of eyes, amazed at the
sudden irruption of this wild-looking individual, were staring
at him coldly.

"What's going on?" said a voice from the other side of the
room.

The cold eyes continued to scrutinize Mark-Alem.

"I'm sorry," he stammered, recoiling. "I do apologize . . ." His brow was covered in perspiration. "Please
forgive me!"

"What *is* going on, Aga Shahin?" said the voice again.

"Nothing of any importance," the other answered. His eyes still fixed on the intruder, he asked: "What do you want?"

Half dead with embarrassment, Mark-Alem opened his mouth to speak, though he wasn't very clear what he was going to say. Fortunately, his hand went to his pocket and encountered the piece of paper with the dream on it.

"I've come to consult the files . . . in the usual way . . . about a dream," he faltered. "But I think I may have come to the wrong door. I'm sorry—it's the first time . . ."

"No, you didn't come to the wrong door."

This was the other voice. At first it had come from behind some shelves, and now Mark-Alem located it for the first time. A familiar face, with bright, smiling eyes, now showed itself.

"You!" murmured Mark-Alem, recalling his first morning and the cafeteria where they'd met. "Do you work here?"

"Yes. So you remember me?" said the other kindly.

"Of course. But I've never seen you again since that first time."

"I saw *you* once when everyone was going home, but you didn't notice me."

"Really? I must have been preoccupied—I'd have liked to . . ."

"You did look rather worried. How's the work going?"

"Quite well."

"Still in Selection?"

"No, I've been transferred to Interpretation."

"Really?" said the other, surprised. "You soon got promoted. Congratulations! I'm really glad."

"Thanks. Is this the Archives?"

"Yes. Did you come to look something up?"

Mark-Alem nodded.

"I'll help you."

The archivist whispered a few words to his colleague, whose hitherto cold eyes now showed a lively curiosity.

"What sector do you want to look in?" asked the archivist.

Mark-Alem shrugged.

"I don't know. This is the first time I've been down here."

"I'll give you a hand."

"I'd be very grateful."

The archivist led the way out of the room.

"I thought I'd meet you again one day," he said as they went along the passage.

"I couldn't find you in the cafeteria."

"No wonder, in all that crowd . . ."

Their footsteps kept time as they walked.

"Do the Archives really take up all this room?" said Mark-Alem, nodding toward the network of passages.

"Yes. It's a real labyrinth. You can easily get lost in it."

"Thank goodness I met you—I don't know what I'd have done otherwise."

"Somebody else would have helped you," replied the archivist.

He walked on in front, while Mark-Alem fretted at not being able to express his gratitude properly.

"Yes, there'd certainly have been somebody else who'd have helped you," said the other. "But I'm going to show you all around the Archives."

"Really?" said Mark-Alem, overwhelmed. "But perhaps you've got things to do—I don't want to be a nuisance."

"Not at all! I'm only too glad to be able to do a little favor for a friend."

Mark-Alem was embarrassed, and didn't know what to say.

"If the Tabir Sarrail is like sleep in comparison with real

life," went on the archivist, opening a door, "the Archives are like a deeper sleep still inside the sleep of the Tabir."

Mark-Alem followed him into an oval-shaped room with walls covered with shelves up to the ceiling.

"There are dozens of rooms like this," said the archivist, pointing to the shelves. "You see these files? There are thousands of them. Tens of thousands."

"And are they all full?"

"Of course," answered the other, leading the way out again. "But we'll go to all the rooms and you can see for yourself."

They were now walking along a narrow passage that seemed to Mark-Alem to slope slightly downward. It was faintly illumined by the light coming from other passages or from the circular corridor.

"Everything is here," said the archivist, slowing down. "What I mean is: If the world were to end—if the earth collided with a comet, say, and were smashed to pieces; or if it evaporated, or disappeared into the abyss—if the globe just vanished leaving no trace but this cellar full of files, that would be enough to show what it used to be like."

The archivist turned around, as if to see what effect his words had had on his companion.

"Do you see what I mean? No history book, no encyclopedia, not all the holy tomes and suchlike put together, nor any school or university or library could supply the truth about our world in so concise and complete a form as these Archives."

"But isn't that truth rather distorted?" Mark-Alem ventured to ask.

The archivist's smile looked even more ironic in profile than it would have done seen full face.

"Who can say it's not what we see with our eyes open that

is distorted, and that what's described here isn't the true essence of things?'' He slowed down outside a door. ''Haven't you ever heard old men sigh that life's a dream?''

He opened the door, and Mark-Alem followed him in. It was an extremely long room, and as in the previous one the walls were covered from floor to ceiling with shelves full of files. One pile was stacked on the floor, apparently for lack of space. Two men were bustling around by the shelves at the far end of the room.

''What's your dream about?'' asked the archivist.

Mark-Alem touched the sheet of paper folded away in his pocket.

''It predicts much loss of life in war.''

''Oh, one of those dreamed just before great slaughter. They're kept in another section, but don't worry—we'll find them. These dreams''—the archivist pointed to the shelves on the left—''are those of the *dark people,* and the dreams opposite are those of the *bright people.*''

Mark-Alem would have liked to ask him what he meant, but didn't like to. He followed him in and out of the narrow passages between the shelves. The other stopped in front of a shelf that was sagging under the weight of all the files on it.

''This is where they keep the dreams about the end of the world according to the inhabitants of places where the winters are very windy.''

He made as if to straighten up the shelf.

''Sometimes,'' he said, ''the people who come down here are very conceited and objectionable. But I like you—you're nice, and it's really a pleasure to show you round.''

''Thank you.''

A low door led off into an adjoining room. The smell of old paper grew more and more pungent, and Mark-Alem was beginning to find it rather difficult to breathe.

"The Resurrection of the Dead . . ." said the archivist. "Allah, the horrors there are here! . . . Well, let's go on a bit. This is Chaos, on all these shelves here—Earth and Heaven all mixed up together. Life-in-death or death-in-life—take your pick. Female life projects. Male life projects . . . Let's go on a bit farther. Erotic dreams—all this room and the adjoining ones are full of them. Economic crises, depreciations, income from land, banks, bankruptcies—all that kind of thing is here. And here are conspiracies, too. Coups d'état nipped in the bud. Government intrigues . . ."

The archivist's voice seemed to be coming from farther and farther away. Sometimes, especially when the two men were in the corridors leading from one room to another, Mark-Alem could scarcely hear what he was saying. The vaulted ceiling sent back a quavering echo.

"And now . . . ow . . . ow . . . we're going to see . . . ee . . . ee . . . the dreams about imprisonment . . . ment . . . ment . . ."

Every time a door creaked, Mark-Alem shuddered.

"Dreams of the first period of captivity . . ." said the archivist, indicating the relevant shelves, "or as they're also called, dreams of early captivity, to distinguish them from the later ones, the dreams of deep imprisonment. The two kinds are very different. In the same way as first loves are different from later ones. And from here to the end of the room are the files containing the really wild imaginings."

Really wild imaginings . . . Mark-Alem couldn't take his eyes off the shelves. How long would he go on wandering through this inferno?

"Yesterday the Master-Dream officers were down here researching till late at night," the archivist told him, lowering his voice. "There's nothing surprising about that. All the great disasters are gathered together here, beginning with what some peoples have recently taken to calling 'national renaissance.' This refers, you understand, not to the resurrection of a dead person, but to that of a whole nation—the sort of thing one daren't even name. . . . Dreams dreamed on the eve of bloodshed, you said?''

"Yes, that's right.''

"Here are the files on that. Most of them are dreams dreamed on the eve of battles, some of them just before dawn. . . . The battle of Kerk-Kili . . . The battle of Bayazit Yeldrum, against Tamburlaine. The two Hungarian campaigns . . .''

"Is the battle of Kosovo here?'' asked Mark-Alem faintly.

The archivist looked up.

"You mean the first, in 1389, against all the Balkans, if I'm not mistaken?''

"Yes, that's right.''

"It's bound to be there. Wait a moment.''

He turned and disappeared among the groaning shelves, evidently to look for the assistant on duty in this section. He soon came back with him.

"This is where they keep the seven hundred or so dreams about it, dreams dreamed on the eve of the fateful day,'' said the archivist, glancing alternately at Mark-Alem and the assistant, whose head, with its emaciated features, nodded in agreement with every word he said.

"There should have been more of them, but they've probably been lost,'' said the assistant in a piping voice. "What's more, a lot of those that are left are very sketchy, as dreams scribbled down in the early hours may well be.''

"Really?'' exclaimed Mark-Alem eagerly.

He'd often heard his family speak of the tragic battle.

"The Master-Dream itself was chosen in haste, so that it could be brought to the Sultan's tent at daybreak.''

"Did they have time to choose a Master-Dream?" asked Mark-Alem, amazed.

"Of course. How could they do otherwise?"

"And is it here?"

"No, it's kept with the others in the Master-Dreams office."

"We'll be going there too—don't worry," said the archivist.

"I can describe it to you more or less," said the assistant, his voice thinner than ever. "Only if you're interested, of course . . ."

"Yes, of course!"

The archivist looked at him briefly and lowered his eyes sympathetically. How could you not be interested, his expression said, seeing that you're a Quprili.

"A soldier dreamed he saw a friend of his who'd been killed sometime before, and the friend beckoned him over behind an embankment. 'What are you doing there all on your own?' said the friend. 'Aren't you bored? Why don't you come and join us? Most of us are over here. . . .' " The assistant related this in a voice that really did seem to come from beyond the grave. "That meant that the battle would be particularly bloody—as indeed it was."

"No, it was certainly no joke," put in the archivist. "The whole Balkan army was wiped out."

Mark-Alem looked from one of his interlocutors to the other.

"Even now, after five centuries, the Balkan peoples often dream of that battle," said the assistant. "Or so I was told by a friend of mine who works on the *'dark people.'* "

"It's quite understandable," observed the archivist, his eyes fixed on Mark-Alem.

"Do you want us to open the files?" asked the assistant.

"No, not now," said the archivist. "We'll come back in a little while, won't we?" He turned to his young companion. "Let's take a look at the Archives as a whole, and then you can come back here and stay as long as you like."

Mark-Alem agreed.

They went back into the passage. The archivist's voice was accompanied by an echo again.

"Now . . . ow . . . ow . . . we're going to see . . . oo see . . . oo see . . . the Ottoman . . . an . . . an . . . archaeo-dreams . . . eams . . . eams. . . ."

"What are they?" asked Mark-Alem after they'd gone through a door and the archivist's voice sounded normal again.

"Old Ottoman dreams," he answered. "The earliest dreams of the founders of the Empire. Hence archaeo-dreams."

"Have they been preserved?"

"Up to a point," said the archivist. "To the same extent as ancient murals can be. They're here in these files."

Mark-Alem made a little bow to the silent clerk who had appeared from between the shelves.

"There aren't very many of them, which makes them all the more valuable," the archivist went on. "But as a matter of fact they've come down to us in such a mutilated form that it isn't possible to learn much from them. Although there have been a number of attempts to restore them, like old frescoes, they're still more or less what they always were—disjointed visions, without any connections between them. Nevertheless, they're sacred, inasmuch as they served as the basis of the State. The present interpreters often come down and look at them, to get inspiration from the way they were explained. Isn't that right, Fouzoul?" he asked the clerk.

"That's right," said the other. "Several of them were here till quite late last night."

"Interpreters from our section?" inquired Mark-Alem.

"From the Master-Dream office. Is that where you work?"

Mark-Alem blushed.

"No—I'm in Interpretation."

"The Master-Dream officers seem to have been everywhere last night," observed the archivist—rather pointedly, Mark-Alem thought. "Thank you, Fouzoul."

He led the way out.

"It's hard to get any meaning out of the archaeo-dreams, even after they've been restored," he said. "I've seen some of them, and they struck me as completely washed-out, like old tapestries where you can't make out the picture anymore. Yet the interpreters spend hours and hours poring over them."

The archivist laughed to himself.

"But I'd bet you anything they don't understand a thing! They just stay there pretending to rack their brains trying to find hidden meanings, and all the time what they're really doing is thinking about their little problems at home, the inadequacy of their salaries, and so on. Ah, here are the Master-Dreams at last!"

Mark-Alem shuddered as though his companion had shown him a nest of vipers—only these had spent their venom long ago. Even so, they still seemed fearsome.

"There are about forty thousand of them altogether," sighed the archivist. "Allah!"

Mark-Alem sighed too.

"And now," said the other, "let's go and see the Sovereign's dreams."

Mark-Alem expected to find a room that was particularly

impressive, but it was just the same as the rest. There was nothing special about the shelves and so on; the only difference was that the files had the Emperor's seal on the cover. Above the seal was written the name of each Sovereign: *Dreams of Sultan Murat I; Dreams of Sultan Bajazet; Dreams of Sultan Mehmet II; Dreams of Sultan Solyman the Magnificent . . .*

"These files can be opened only on the Sovereign's orders," said the archivist. "Anyone breaking the rule has his head cut off."

He drew the edge of his hand across his throat.

They went on and visited rooms containing dreams of the *giaours* and of profound captivity. Also others devoted to anxieties (there were three big rooms full of those) and to hallucinations (there had been long debates about whether or not they really ought to be examined in the Tabir Sarrail at all). In the last room were the dreams of the insane.

"Well, I think you've got some idea of the Archives now," said the archivist as they left.

Mark-Alem looked at him with eyes that seemed to implore pity.

Then he and his companion went back to the shelves where the file on the battle of Kosovo was kept. And there they parted.

"When you've finished," said the archivist, "go along this corridor until you reach the circular one. There you can turn either way—you'll come to a staircase whichever direction you take."

The assistant on duty offered Mark-Alem a small table and put the file he wanted in front of him. With trembling fingers Mark-Alem started turning the ancient pages; they were made of a heavy kind of paper that had long ago fallen into disuse. Most had stains all over them, and the ink was so faded that many words were almost illegible. Mark-Alem felt a sudden pain in the head, as if someone had hit him with an ax. He had spots before his eyes. He shut them for a moment to rest them, then opened them again. Then he started to read, but very slowly, unable to concentrate. Something seemed to be keeping the meaning of the text at a distance from his brain, making it vibrate like the echo of the archivist's voice in the vaulted corridors. But he forced himself to persevere. The language was ancient, and many of the words were incomprehensible. Above all, the order of the words in the sentences seemed very unnatural—a real jumble. But he had to make do with what he'd got. This was the first time he'd ever consulted texts as old as this, dating from some five centuries ago. Gradually, encouraged by deciphering a bit of meaning here and there, he found himself progressing more easily. Most of the dreams were described very briefly, in two or three lines, some in just one, and this made the going less difficult than he'd thought it would be at first. If it hadn't been for the interpretations underneath the texts, he could have read the whole file in a few hours.

Mark-Alem felt his fatigue disappear. His eyes were gradually getting used to the outmoded characters, and he was beginning to find the strange syntax amusing. Little by little the skimpy, mutilated lines drew him into their own universe. His imagination was filled with a vision of the plain of Kosovo in northern Albania, where he had never set foot: a dreamlike and confused vision, the combined product of several hundred drowsy brains. And as if this weren't enough, these vague and meaningless visions were accompanied by interpretations which made them even more difficult to grasp. Yet, perhaps because of the common anxiety felt by all the dreamers on the brink of that fatal day, and perhaps because this anguish was shared by those appointed to scribble them down, the motley collection of individual dreams possessed a curious unity. Before dawn, when the plain was still wet only with dew, in the minds of the sleeping soldiers it had filled with pools of blood which grew thicker and darker as night fell. Into the earlier pools flowed new streams of blood, soon to grow gradually darker, but never dark enough to be indistinguishable from the old. Then, at dusk, the end of the fighting, with the defeat of the Balkan allies and the murder of the Sultan just as he was rejoicing in victory. Then came the Sultan's tent, where his body was taken, his death kept hidden from the army; the secret meeting of the Viziers; the dispatch of a messenger to fetch Jakub Tchelebi, one of the Sultan's two sons. "Come, your glorious father has sent for you. . . ." The prince entering the tent, thinking his father had really summoned him, and then his own murder, hacked to death in cold blood by the Viziers to avoid a power struggle between the two brothers . . .

Mark-Alem rubbed his eyes as if there were a mist veiling his sight. What was the truth, then? Could it ever be found when its very roots were in dream? What's more, there was no clear frontier between the dream and the reality. Everything to do with the battle on the plain—the lie of the land, the bad weather, the different incidents, the eyewitness accounts—all was confused and tangled. The white souls of three hundred thousand Balkan soldiers in their last agonies formed a vast blizzard swirling over the earth. Why was the Great Sultan running wildly through the flying snowflakes as if to flee with them? "Where are you going, Padishah? Pull yourself together!" Selim the janissary had cried out in his sleep, and on waking had hastened to tell of his dream. Further on, Prince Jakub Tchelebi, drenched in blood, ran across the plain in the form of a maneless horse. And here again were pools of blood, summer, winter, the seasons intermingled, with the plain covered simultaneously with rain and sunshine, snow and greenery, flowers and icy desolation. It would have to rain for weeks, months, to wash away all that blood. And the snow would have to come and turn everything white for all that suffering to seem to be covered over. But next spring, when little streams began to trickle through the spotless drifts, they would carry little clots of blood along with them, as if the snow itself had been wounded. And that is why, O Allah, in any kind of weather, winter or summer, in wind or silent rain, that plain there in northern Albania . . .

Mark-Alem suddenly remembered that he and his mother were invited to the Vizier's house that evening. It was the night of the traditional dinner party when they listened to the Balkan bards. This time, as well as the Bosnians, there'd undoubtedly be the Albanese rhapsodists Kurt had invited.

Mark-Alem shut the files and stood up. His head ached from reading too much, or perhaps because of the coal fumes, which were worse in the basement than on the higher floors. He nodded at the assistants on duty and left. His footsteps echoed along the corridor. What time could it be? He had no idea. At ground level it could easily be lunchtime, or the middle of the afternoon, or perhaps evening. For a moment he felt quite anxious: What if he was late for dinner? But he soon stopped worrying. The time couldn't have gone by as fast as that. The dinner seemed to belong to a different universe somewhere up above, almost in the clouds, while down here, to right and left of him, behind the blank walls of the corridors, in thousands upon thousand of files, lay the sleep of the whole world. He could feel his eyelids drooping. What's happening? he thought. What was this somnolence that was creeping over him? For a moment he was terrified, but then he told himself it must be the effect of the coal fumes. . . . "What are you doing here all on your own? Why don't you come and join us? Most of us are over here. . . ."

Mark-Alem mended his pace so as to get to the circular corridor as fast as possible, but it still didn't appear. The farther he went the more lost he felt. What if he collapsed and lost consciousness in these empty corridors? Again he felt his eyelids growing heavy. Why on earth did I ever come down here? he asked himself. He began to walk so fast he was almost running. The sound of his own footsteps, multiplied by the echo, increased his terror. I will *not* go to sleep! he told himself. No, I won't fall into your trap!

Heaven knows how long he would have rushed along like that if a man hadn't suddenly appeared in front of him at an intersection.

"What's the matter?" asked the stranger anxiously.

"Nothing," said Mark-Alem. "Where's the way out?"

"But you look so pale—have you heard what happened?"

"What? I'm just looking for the way out. . . ."

"I wondered if you'd heard anything. You're as white as a sheet. . . ."

"Perhaps it's the fumes. . . ."

"I just thought . . ."

"How can I get out of here?"

"This way," said the other.

Mark-Alem was tempted to say, "But you look pale too—why are you so upset about me?" But he didn't want to lingèr even for a moment. Let me get out of this hole as soon as possible, he groaned inwardly.

At last he spied the stairs, and sped up them three if not four at a time. As he paused on the ground floor, out of breath, he thought he heard a sound. When he turned around he was astonished to see a group of men in long capes vanishing in the distance down the corridor.

On the second floor he passed another group, a bunch of gloomy-looking individuals. The sound of footsteps came from the other corridors. What were all these comings and goings? he wondered, and he thought again of the man he'd met in the corridor down by the Archives. Something must be going on in the Palace. He hurried on, eager to get back to Interpretation. From the dreariness beyond the window-panes he could tell that daylight was fading.

"Where've you been all day?" asked his neighbor, back in the office.

"I was down in the Archives."

The other stared. It was only a week since he'd been put to work next to Mark-Alem, but that was long enough to show him that the newcomer was addicted to gossip, especially whispered political gossip, clandestine and dangerous— the more dangerous the better. It was strange he hadn't yet found out that Mark-Alem was a Quprili.

"There's something going on," said this fellow, leaning over close to Mark-Alem. "Can't you feel it?"

Mark-Alem shrugged.

"I noticed some stir in the corridors. But that's all I know," he answered shortly.

"The head of the section was sent for three times, and each time he came back looking terrified. They've just sent for him again, but he isn't back yet."

"What can it be about?"

"Who can say? It might be anything."

Mark-Alem almost told him about the frightened-looking man he'd seen in the basement, but that would only have unleashed a flood of whispering. He remembered what the archivist had said about the Master-Dream officers working all night in the Archives. Yes, there was definitely something going on.

"It might be anything," whispered his neighbor. To avoid attracting attention he kept his head still and spoke out of the corner of his mouth. "Anything, from the sacking of some officials to the closing down of the Palace itself."

"The closing down of the Tabir Sarrail?"

"Why not? With all this upset . . . these strange comings and goings in the corridors . . . I've worked here for years; I know the ways of the place by now. And I don't like the look of what's been going on today. After that, anything can happen. . . ."

"Has the Tabir ever been closed?" quavered Mark-Alem.

"What a question!" muttered the other. "Woe betide us if that happens! . . . As a matter of fact, I have known certain dark periods when the Sovereign issued a special decree suspending the analysis of dreams. But that happens only rarely, very rarely, you know. When it does, the only dreams that are studied are those of the Sovereign. Then it's as if the Tabir Sarrail had gone into mourning. You'd think it was some sort of ruin, with the staff roaming round the corridors like souls in torment. Everything seems on the point of giving up the ghost. Everyone just waits, chilled to the bone, for the day to end. And from that state of affairs to the closing down of the Tabir, it's only a stone's throw. . . ."

Mark-Alem could feel a lump creeping up from his stomach to his throat. He vaguely remembered what the Vizier had said. Wasn't this the eventuality he'd hinted at, without wanting to put it into words? His neighbor droned on, but Mark-Alem had stopped listening. His head was thudding fit to burst, his thoughts were inextricably confused. . . . In the course of his endless conversations with the Vizier, not to mention their last interview, he'd got the idea that the worse things were for the Palace of Dreams, the better they would be for the Quprilis. So the unluckier today proved to be for the Tabir, the more reason he himself ought to have to rejoice. But it wasn't like that at all. The uncertainty all around him, far from giving him pleasure, only made him more afraid.

He listened to his neighbor's mumblings, but could scarcely make out a word. The other man seemed to be talking to himself. Mark-Alem remembered asking his grandmother one day: "Grandma, why do you talk to yourself?" And she answered: "To pretend there's two of us, dear. So as not to feel lonely. . . ." Mark-Alem felt like heaving a sigh, as his grandmother had done then. They were all so lonely, sitting totally cut off from one another at cold desks strewn with crazy visions conjured up by the minds of strangers. . . .

"But why?" said Mark-Alem faintly, interrupting the other's babble. "Why is it happening?"

"Why is it happening?" The twisted lips of his neighbor seemed to aim at Mark-Alem not words but an icy grin. "My God, how can anyone ever ask 'Why?' in this place? Can you ever find out the reason for anything here?"

Mark-Alem sighed. The windowpanes were quite dark now. Night had fallen. The light from the lamps cast a feeble glow on the brows bent over their desks.

"Hey, here comes the boss," said his neighbor. "Back at last."

Mark-Alem glanced where the other was pointing.

"He doesn't look as upset as all that to me," he whispered.

"Doesn't he?" Then, after a pause: "No, you're right. He looks better to me too. Let's hope there's good news."

Mark-Alem felt a pang of anxiety.

"He looks quite pleased, actually."

"I wouldn't go as far as that. But he doesn't look as worried as he did."

"Roll on the end of the day!" said Mark-Alem, gazing at his boss. He thought he saw a feverish gleam in his eye. "God help us!"

"The day will end all right," said his neighbor. "But shall *we* be able to go home?"

"What do you mean?"

"On a day like this we might well have to stay here all night."

Mark-Alem remembered he was supposed to be going to the Vizier's that evening, and was about to mention the fact to his neighbor. Anyhow, he thought, I can ask permission to go. Surely they wouldn't dare prevent him from going to dinner with his influential uncle? He rubbed his forehead with the palm of his hand. What if all this were just imagination? After all, they were only talking about suppositions with no foundation yet in fact. The people in the corridor, the changing expressions of the head of the section—that wasn't much to go on! That neighbor of his was crazy. Mark-Alem didn't know how he could have let himself get carried away by his maunderings.

The bell for the end of work made him start. Mark-Alem's eyes met those of his neighbor, and he almost shouted, "You see, you idiot—you got me all worked up for nothing! It's just a day like any other—there's the bell ringing at the usual time. What did you want to go and frighten me like that for?"

The other was the first to close his file; then he hurried out with a glance at Mark-Alem that seemed to say, "You get off too while you've got the chance!"

Mark-Alem followed. The corridors and stairs were swarming with people, and the thud of anonymous footsteps seemed to shake the building to its foundations. He added his own to the rest, with the relief of a frightened man hiding himself in a crowd. Two or three times he got the feeling that it was just an ordinary end to a day, but immediately afterward he felt the opposite. He looked at the other people out of the corner of his eye, and thought he could see a flush on their cheeks reflecting some deep inner fever. Not just ordinary excitement, but a seething impatience at the prospect of the unknown. Rubbish, he told himself. There's nothing of the kind in those faces drawn with fatigue and worn out by the ravings of dreams. It's my own nerves that are to blame. . . .

When he got outside the building he extricated himself from the crowd, and the farther away he got from them, the more absurd his apprehensions seemed. It's that madman that got me down, he thought. The scene between the two of them was really comical.

He looked for a cab, to get home more quickly. He didn't want to be late for that dinner. He put his hand up two or three times, but either because they didn't notice him or because they were engaged, the drivers didn't stop. Mark-Alem wasn't the sort of person to stand on the curb and shout, "Hey, cabby!" He preferred to walk, even if it was raining or snowing, rather than call attention to himself. Luckily there weren't as many pedestrians as usual, so he got along quite fast. If it was like this all the way home he'd have time to change and perhaps have a bath before dinner.

Lost in thought, he had almost forgotten his recent fears when something—he didn't realize exactly what it was at first—a gasp of surprise, a rapid footfall, a whisper?—made him look up and glance toward the crossroads. Two patrols were stationed in the middle, looking at the passersby suspiciously. What was going on? Before he had time to hazard a guess, he caught sight of another patrol a little farther on, and then another. There were soldiers everywhere. The anguish he thought he'd left behind at the door of the Palace of Dreams now swept over him again. The other people in the streets were also peering unobtrusively at the patrols. Some turned around for a last look as they walked away.

After he'd gone on for a while without seeing any more uniforms, Mark-Alem thought, Perhaps it's only a coincidence? People were going in and out of the little taverns scattered along the street, and there didn't seem to be any sign of alarm anywhere. And there was the café called The Nights of Ramadan, with music coming out of it as usual. Yes, he said to himself for the umpteenth time, it must be a coincidence. Anyhow, hadn't he seen patrols there before? He could even remember they'd been there then to check people's identity. Yes, obviously a coincidence. The Central Bank was close by; who knows, perhaps they were expecting an attempt at armed robbery and were taking precautions.

It seemed to Mark-Alem there were more sentries than usual outside the Ministry of Finance, but he didn't have the heart to look and make sure. The streetlamps shed a sinister light. He mumbled, "To the devil with all of them!"—not sure whom he meant. The trembling he'd tried to repress had returned. By the time he reached the Palace of the Sheikh-ul-Islam he was sure this unusual activity owed nothing to chance, and something really was going on. A large group of soldiers and policemen, almost half a battalion, was massed outside the wrought-iron railings. "There's something going on," he muttered. Something . . . But what? A plot? An attempted coup d'état? A siege? He wanted to hasten on, but couldn't. His legs felt like cotton. Hurry up, he told himself, but he knew all effort was useless. He thought of the dinner, and of the old custom, which was even mentioned in the epic, that decreed that a Quprili never canceled a dinner party.

On the Crescent Bridge he saw more helmeted soldiers, but he was now in such a state that nothing could affect him either way. At last he reached his own street with its somber chestnut trees, and saw lights on the second floor of his house. He could make out the shape of a vehicle outside the gate and, as he drew near, saw the letter Q carved on the carriage door. He heaved a sigh of relief and went in.

THE DINNER

...

vi.

At first, so as not to worry his mother, Mark-Alem didn't mention his doubts, but an hour later, as they were getting into the carriage to go to the Vizier's, he couldn't help saying:

"There was a certain amount of agitation at the Palace today."

"What!" she said, gripping his hand. "Agitation? Why?"

"I couldn't find out anything definite. But on the way home I passed a lot of patrols."

He felt his mother's hand tremble against his own, and was sorry he'd spoken.

"But perhaps it's nothing at all," he reassured her. "Perhaps they're just rumors."

"But what did you hear?" she asked in a choked voice.

"Oh, silly things!" he said, trying to sound casual. "It seems the Sovereign sent back yesterday's Master-Dream. But perhaps the story's not true. There could be quite a different explanation for the unusual activity."

The noise of the carriage wheels breaking the silence was unbearable.

"If the Sovereign really did send the Master-Dream back, that's not unimportant," said Mark-Alem's mother.

"But there really may be nothing to it."

"That only makes it worse. It means that what's going on is more disturbing still."

I shouldn't have told her anything, though Mark-Alem.

"But what could it be that's more disturbing?"

His mother sighed.

"How can we tell? I don't know much about what you do in that place. You've mentioned the possibility of mistaken interpretations and sudden inspections. Mark, tell me the truth—you haven't got mixed up in anything wrong, have you?"

He tried to laugh.

"Me? I really don't know anything about all this, I swear. I spent the whole of today down in the Archives. It was only when I came back upstairs that I heard that something was going on."

Through the noise of the wheels he heard his mother fetch another deep sigh, then murmur, "God help us!"

He could just see, through the carriage windows and in the pallid light of the streetlamps, the dark buildings to the right and the left of the road, and here and there a few pedestrians. What if the dinner has been put off? thought Mark-Alem. The closer they got to the Vizier's palace, the more the thought obsessed him. But he comforted himself with the reflection that this was all the more unlikely because the occasion was connected with the family epic, and thus with the very foundations of the Quprili dynasty. No, it couldn't possibly have been put off. To tell the truth, he wasn't sure whether he wanted it to be canceled or not. Anyhow, when he saw the lights by the palace gate and the guests' carriages drawn up along the pavement, he felt relieved. It seemed to him his mother sighed too, as if a weight had been lifted from her shoulders. There were the Vizier's guards standing by the gates as usual, and everything else as it always was on such occasions: lighted torches lining the path from the gate to the steps leading up to the front door; the majordomo standing in the entrance; the hall filled with a pleasant smell of mint. You felt it was impossible for the anxieties of the day just ending to pass through the gates of the palace.

Mark-Alem and his mother went into the main drawing room. From two silver braziers in the middle of the room came a comfortable warmth that consorted well with the dark red of the carpets and the gentle hum of conversation.

The guests included a few close cousins, all in high positions, several old family friends, the Austrian consul's son—a tall fair youth to whom Kurt was talking in French—and two or three other people whom Mark-Alem hadn't met before. He heard his mother quietly ask a footman where the Vizier was, and the man said he was upstairs but would be down soon. Mark-Alem felt calmer now. The icy dread that had gripped him all the evening like some dank and baneful mist was fading away.

The footmen were serving *raki* in silver goblets. Through

the buzz of talk Mark-Alem tried to hear what Uncle Kurt and
the Austrian were saying in French. After downing a glass of
raki in one gulp, he felt a wave of euphoria. When, after a
moment, his eyes met those of his mother, he quickly looked
away. She seemed to be saying, "What was all that nonsense
you were telling me just now?"

The entrance of the Vizier immediately struck a chill into
the atmosphere. This wasn't so much because of his gloomy
expression—most of those present were accustomed to
that—as because he also looked preoccupied and gazed at his
guests as if he were surprised to see them there and were
waiting for them to tell him why they had come. After saying
good evening he stood by one of the braziers, holding his
hands spread over it to warm them. To Mark-Alem the rings
around his eyes looked even darker than on the evening of
their memorable dinner.

Kurt, evidently feeling it was up to him to try to restore
an air of normality to the proceedings, went over to his
brother and whispered a few words which Mark-Alem
couldn't hear. But they must have had to do with the Austrian, for the Vizier replied to Kurt and the other young man
at the same time, and the Austrian nodded respectfully as
Kurt translated his brother's words. After this, things did
seem a little more relaxed. The guests began to converse in
pairs, while the Austrian went on talking to the Vizier with
Kurt still acting as interpreter. Mark-Alem was tempted to
move nearer to listen, but one of his cousins, the bald one
who'd had supper with them the day before Mark-Alem
started work in the Palace of Dreams, asked in a whisper:

"How are you getting on at the Tabir?"

"Very well," said Mark-Alem, though his mouth turned
down at the corners to indicate only "So-so."

"Are you working in Interpretation?"

He nodded. A gleam of irony came into his cousin's expression, but Mark-Alem didn't care. He had eyes for no one but his favorite uncle, Kurt. He'd never seen him looking so handsome and elegant, in his immaculate white starched collar which cast a magical glow over his face. Mark-Alem was soon convinced that the mainspring of the whole evening was Kurt, who had had the strange idea of inviting the Albanian rhapsodists. Mark-Alem was eager to hear at last the Albanian version of the family epic, until now as unknown to them as the other side of the moon.

Someone who was evidently the last of the guests now entered, apologizing for his late arrival:

"There's a certain amount of unusual activity outside," he said. "The forces of law and order are checking people's identity."

Some of the guests tried to catch the Vizier's eye, but he seemed quite unaffected by the latecomer's words. He must know what's going on, thought Mark-Alem. Otherwise he wouldn't take the news with such indifference. The Vizier didn't seem to have noticed his nephew either; it was as if he'd completely forgotten the disjointed conversation they'd had that evening a few weeks before. Only an hour ago Mark-Alem had been wondering whether he oughtn't to tell the Vizier what had happened at the Tabir Sarrail. Hadn't the moment come for him to be on his guard? But now, seeing his uncle so unconcerned, Mark-Alem felt reassured too.

That being so, he began to examine the patterns in the huge Persian carpet, the largest and most beautiful he'd ever seen, a birthday present to the Vizier from the Sovereign. It was one of the few things that still seemed to him as lovely as ever, though since he'd started working in the Palace of Dreams the rest of the world had grown pale and dull.

He only raised his eyes from the carpet when he realized

that everyone had suddenly fallen silent. The Vizier was preparing to speak. He told his guests that they were about to hear the rhapsodists from Albania; then, during and after dinner, as was the custom, the Slav rhapsodists would sing passages from the Quprili epic.

"Show them in," he told the majordomo.

After a while the rhapsodists entered, amid a complete silence. There were three of them, dressed in typical native costume. Two of them were middle-aged, one of them slightly younger, and each was carrying his fragile stringed instrument. Mark-Alem's attention was immediately captured by these instruments—*lahutas*, as they were called. They were very like the *guslas* of the Slav rhapsodists, and Mark-Alem felt the same surprise, not to say disappointment, as he'd experienced when he first saw the *guslas*. Having heard so much about the famous epic, he'd imagined that the instruments accompanying it would somehow be as strange, weighty, majestic, and imposing as the chant itself, and that the rhapsodists would have to drag them along behind them. But the *gusla* was merely a simple wooden instrument with a single string, and could easily be carried in one hand. It had seemed incredible that this wretched thing could bring the vast ancient epic to life. And now Mark-Alem had seen the *lahuta*, his disappointment was even more acute. Ever since he'd heard Kurt talking about the Albanian version of their epic, he'd for some reason thought the Albanian *lahuta* would cure the shock that the *gusla* had administered to his imagination. He'd expected it to be not only heavy and impressive but also steeped in the blood he associated in his mind with the cruelty of their epic. But it had turned out to be as rudimentary as the *gusla*—just a wooden sounding box with an opening on top and one solitary string.

By now the rhapsodists were standing between the two

groups into which the guests had of their own accord divided themselves. The bards had fair hair, and their bright eyes seemed to express not so much scorn as complete rejection of anything that might be offered them.

The footmen had served them *raki* in the same kind of silver goblets as those they'd handed round to the other guests, but the Albanians merely touched them with their lips.

"Well, you can begin," said the Vizier in Albanian.

One of the rhapsodists sat down on a stool which the majordomo had brought. He laid his *lahuta* on his lap, then sat for a moment looking at the string. Then he lifted his bow in his right hand and laid it across the string. The first sounds were faint and monotonous, tending obstinately back to their point of departure. It was like a long, too long, stifling lament. If it goes on like this, thought Mark-Alem, everyone will be gasping for air. When was the fellow going to start on the words? Everyone else was obviously wondering the same thing. This kind of music needed to be padded with words; otherwise this string would scrape their souls raw.

When the rhapsodist finally opened his mouth and began to sing, Mark-Alem was at first relieved. But there was something inhuman about the man's voice, too. It was as if some strange operation had been performed on it, removing all everyday tones and leaving only eternal ones. It was a voice in which the throat of man and the throat of the mountains seemed, over ages, to have attuned themselves to one another and merged. And so with other voices, ever more distant, until they all joined in the lament of the stars. Words and voice alike might as easily have come from the mouth of the dead as of the living. Another accord—the closest and the most perfect—had been made with the shades of the dead.

Mark-Alem couldn't take his eyes off the slender, solitary string stretched across the sounding box. It was the string that secreted the lament; the box amplified it to terrifying proportions. Suddenly it was revealed to Mark-Alem that this hollow cage was the breast containing the soul of the nation to which he belonged. It was from there that the vibrant age-old lament arose. He'd already heard fragments of it; only today would he be permitted to hear the whole. He now felt the hollow of the *lahuta* inside his own breast.

Then another rhapsodist started to sing "The Ballad of the Bridge," and through the hush that surrounded it, Mark-Alem seemed to hear the blows of the masons, building in the cold sunshine a bridge sullied with the blood of sacrifice. A bridge that would not only give the Quprili family its name but would also mark them with its own doom.

Though his chest was constricted with tension, Mark-Alem suddenly felt an almost irresistible desire to discard "Alem," the Asian half of his first name, and appear with a new one, one used by the people of his native land: Gjon, Gjergj, or Gjorg.

Mark-Gjon, Mark-Gjergj Ura, Mark-Gjorg Ura, he repeated, as if trying to get used to his new half name, every time he heard the word "Ura," the only one of the rhapsodist's words he could understand.

Suddenly there came back to him the dream of a certain merchant, about a musical instrument heard in the middle of some wasteland. He couldn't remember the details—only that he'd felt like throwing it into the wastepaper basket at first but then had let it pass. And now it seemed to him that the musical instrument described in the dream bore a strange resemblance to the *lahuta*.

The rhapsodist went on singing in the same resonant voice. Kurt gazed fixedly at him; his eyes were shining feverishly. Every so often, in a whisper, he translated a passage, a few verses, to the Austrian, who was also listening intently. The

Vizier stood motionless, the rings under his eyes darker than ever, his hands folded in front of him. Mark-Alem could get the drift of a few lines here and there, but most of them were unintelligible.

*Thou hast found a grave, O thou, bound by the bessa!**

Almost imperceptibly he moved nearer to where his young uncle and the Austrian were. Kurt was just trying to translate that line. Mark-Alem, who understood a little French, listened.

"It's extremely difficult to translate," Kurt was saying. "Almost impossible, in fact . . ."

Mark-Alem did his best to follow the text of the epic, partly through what he could make out for himself and partly by listening to Kurt's translation.

"It's about a man trying to challenge his dead enemy to a duel on his grave," Kurt explained to the Austrian. "Rather macabre, eh?"

"Magnificent!" replied the other.

"The dead man can't get up, and he struggles and groans," Kurt went on.

My God, thought Mark-Alem suddenly, it's all quite clear! And indeed it couldn't be plainer. The sounding box of the *lahuta* was the grave in which the dead man was struggling. His groans, arising from below, were uniquely terrifying.

"And now here are the owls, birds of ill omen," whispered Kurt.

The Austrian nodded agreement as his friend spoke.

"This is the knight, Zuk, treacherously blinded by his mother and her lover, who wanders over the snowy mountains on his blinded steed."

"Blinded by his mother! My God!" exclaimed the Aus-

*Promise

trian. "But it's like the *Oresteia! Das ist die Orestiaden!*"

Mark-Alem was now quite close to them, so as not to miss a word of what they said. Kurt was just about to go on with his commentary when there was a sudden noise. Heads turned in all directions, some toward the doors, some toward the windows. Then the noise came again, mingled with shrill cries, and then amid all the din there was a loud banging at the outer door.

"What is it? What's happening?" cried anxious voices. Then all were silent. The rhapsodist stopped singing. There was another knocking, louder than before.

"My God, what can it be?" gasped someone.

Everyone turned toward the Vizier, whose face had suddenly turned deathly pale. There was a distant sound of a door opening, then a brief cry, followed by the tramp of approaching footsteps. The guests stood petrified, gazing at the drawing-room doors. These were finally shoved open roughly, and a group of armed men appeared on the threshold. Something—perhaps the lights in the room, or the sight of the guests, or the cry that issued from some unknown throat—seemed to stop them in their tracks for a moment. Then one of them came forward, scanned the room apparently without finding what he was looking for, and said:

"The Sovereign's police!"

No one said anything.

"Vizier Quprili?" said the officer, having now evidently found the person he sought. He took a couple of steps toward the Vizier, bowed deeply, and said:

"Excellency, I have orders from the Sovereign. Allow me to execute them."

Then he brought out from his breast a decree, which he proceeded to unfold as the Vizier looked on. His white face didn't change now; it had changed as much as it could already.

The officer took his impassiveness as permission.

"Your papers!" he shouted, turning suddenly to the guests and nodding to his men to enter.

There were about half a dozen of them, all armed, and wearing the badges of the imperial police on their caps and collars.

"I'm a foreign citizen," the voice of the Austrian could be heard protesting amid the rising hubbub.

Mark-Alem looked around in vain for his mother. A voice that was meant to be severe but which tried to avoid brutality was saying at intervals: "This way! This way!"

Someone had opened a side door leading into the adjoining salon, and a group of guests was being herded into it.

"Kurt Quprili!" shouted one of the policemen, pointing Kurt out to his chief. "He's the one."

The officer went over to him, taking some handcuffs out of his pocket on the way.

Mark-Alem saw the officer grab Kurt's wrists adroitly with one hand and fix the handcuffs on them with the other. Strangely enough, Kurt didn't offer the slightest resistance. All he did was look at the handcuffs in surprise. Mark-Alem, like some of the other guests, turned to the Vizier, expecting him to put an end to this absurd scene. But the Vizier's face remained expressionless. Anyone else might have thought the powerful Vizier's failure to respond to an outrage committed under his own roof had something to do with fear. But Mark-Alem guessed there was another reason for his resignation. This was the ancient reflex of the Quprilis, who in similar circumstances, scores of times in the history of their family, assumed the mask of unreality. Its features reflected fatalism, abstraction, and weariness.

Mark-Alem felt like shouting, "Wake up, Uncle, pull yourself together!—don't you see what's happening?" But in the eyes of the Vizier, even while with everyone else he watched Kurt being led out, there was a trace of what looked like submission. You suspected he was really looking into the distance, into some mysterious depths where the official machine that had engendered this misfortune might have been set in motion.

I only hope he's thinking of a way to stop it, thought Mark-Alem, approaching the Vizier in an attempt to see if this were so. And perhaps because he was so close, perhaps by mere chance, their eyes briefly met. In that short time, in the look that sprang as through a rift in his uncle's brow, it seemed to Mark-Alem that he understood the meaning of their previous incomprehensible interview. And suddenly, painfully, he was transfixed by the thought that all this had to do with the Palace of Dreams and with himself, Mark-Alem; and that this time the Quprilis had probably been caught out. . . .

He felt two hands pushing him roughly toward the door into the other room. As he went in he caught a glimpse of the rhapsodists, still standing alone amid a small crowd of guests.

"Mark!" He heard his mother's gentle voice as soon as he entered the smaller salon. He would have expected a cry or a sob, but she sounded almost calm. "What's happening in the other room?"

He shrugged and didn't answer.

"I was worried about you," she whispered. "What misfortune has befallen us now?"

He could see that most of the guests had now moved into this room. Every so often a voice could be heard asking, "What's going on in there? How much longer is this going to last?"

"Have they taken Kurt away?" asked Mark-Alem's mother.

"I think so."

She's keeping herself under control, he thought. She's not a Quprili for nothing. But he noticed she was as white as a sheet.

All of a sudden, through the communicating doors between the two drawing rooms, they could hear piercing cries, followed by a scuffle and a groan.

Mark-Alem made to join those of the guests who were rushing toward the doors, but his mother held him back.

From the other room came more cries, then the sound of a body falling to the floor.

"*Was ist los?*" said the Austrian.

"The doors are locked."

Every face was pale with fear.

Mark-Alem felt his mother's fingers gripping his arm like a vise. From beyond the door came another heartrending cry, cut off short.

"Who was that?" someone asked. "That voice . . ."

"It wasn't the Vizier."

They heard the sound of a body falling heavily, and a terrifying "Ah!"

"My God, what's going on?"

For a few moments everyone was silent. Then, through the silence, a voice said:

"They're murdering the rhapsodists."

Mark-Alem buried his face in his hands. From the other room came the clatter of boots receding in the distance. Someone started twisting the door handles.

"Open up, for the love of God!"

The door into the main drawing room was still locked. But another one opened, onto an inner corridor, and a voice shouted: "This way!"

The guests filed out like shadows, except one who had

fainted and slumped onto a chair. The corridor was feebly lighted and full of the sound of footsteps. "Have they killed Kurt?" asked someone. "No—but they took him away." "This way, ladies and gentlemen," said a valet. "You can get out this way." *"Wo ist Kurt?"*

The little procession of guests came out into the main corridor by the larger drawing room, in which some vague figures could be seen through the frosted glass in the doors. Mark-Alem wrenched free from his mother's grasp and went over to find out what was happening. One of the doors was ajar, and through the gap he could see part of the drawing room. Everything was turned upside down. Then he caught sight of the lifeless bodies of two rhapsodists stretched out close together on the floor. A third corpse lay a little way farther off, near an overturned brazier; its face was half covered with ashes.

The policemen had gone. Only the footmen were left, walking silently over a carpet strewn with broken glass. Mark-Alem caught a glimpse of a motionless image of the Vizier hanging on the wall, and by pushing the door a bit farther open he could see the Vizier himself, still in the same rigid attitude as before. My God, it all happened in front of his very eyes! thought Mark-Alem. And it seemed to him the Vizier's eyes had something in common with the splinters of glass scattered all over the floor.

Suddenly he felt his mother's hand seize him and pull him resolutely toward her. He hadn't the strength to resist. He felt like vomiting.

The hall was almost empty. Through the open front door he could see the lights of the carriages driving away one after the other.

"Everyone else has gone," breathed his mother almost inaudibly. "What are *we* going to do?"

He didn't answer.

One of the footmen put out the center lights. Beyond the doors of the main drawing room, still the same silent coming and going. After a few minutes the footmen brought out the corpses of the rhapsodists, carrying them by their arms and legs. The face of the third, the one that was half covered with ashes, looked particularly horrible. Mark-Alem's mother turned her head away. He himself was hard put to it not to vomit, but despite everything, he felt he couldn't leave. The last footman came out with the musical instruments. Soon afterward all the servants went back into the drawing room.

"What shall we do?" whispered Mark-Alem's mother.

He didn't know what to answer.

The drawing-room doors were now wide open, and they could see the footmen rolling up the bloodstained carpet.

"I can't go on looking at this much longer," she said. "It's too much for me."

They were putting out the lights in the drawing room, too, now. Mark-Alem looked around, incapable of making any decision. The other guests must all be gone by now. Perhaps he and his mother would do well to leave too? But perhaps they ought to stay, as near relatives usually do when there's a misfortune in the family. Even if they wanted to go home they couldn't have done so. They lived a long way away—too far to walk, especially on a night like this. As for finding a cab, there was no point in even thinking about it.

Most of the lights were out now. Just a few lamps were left burning here and there on the stairs and in the corridors. The huge house grew full of whispers. A few flunkeys came and went like shadows, carrying candlesticks which cast yellow gleams along the passages.

Mark-Alem's mother groaned from time to time. "My God—what was that ghastly business?"

After a while a door creaked and the Vizier emerged out of the shadows of the drawing room. Moving slowly, like a sleepwalker, he went straight up the darkened staircase.

Mark-Alem's mother touched his hand.

"The Vizier! Did you see him?"

A few moments later a footman hurtled down the stairs and out of the front door. Almost at once they heard the sound of a carriage driving rapidly away.

Mark-Alem and his mother stayed for some time in the semidarkness, watching the little flames of candles being carried hither and thither. No one bothered about them. In silence they went out of the front door, which had been left ajar, and made their way to the tall iron gate. The sentries were still on duty. Mark-Alem didn't have a very clear idea of the way home. His mother remembered even less, having always made the journey in a closed carriage.

After an hour they were still walking, and beginning to wonder if they were lost. Soon they heard the sound of carriage wheels approaching fast. They flattened themselves against the wall to let the vehicle pass, and as it did so Mark-Alem thought he saw a Q carved on one of its doors.

"I believe that was the Vizier's carriage," he whispered. "Perhaps the same one that set out a little while ago."

His mother didn't answer. She was shivering in the cold and damp.

A short time later another carriage brushed by them equally impetuously, and although there were no street lights, Mark-Alem thought he saw the letter Q again. Despite the darkness he even waved his arms in the hope that the carriage would stop and drive them home. But it galloped off into the mist. Mark-Alem concluded it was foolish to expect help from anyone tonight, this night of anguish full of capital Qs swooping by like birds of ill omen.

*   *   *

It *was long* past midnight when they reached home at last. Loke, who'd had a presentiment that something was wrong, was still up. They gave her a brief account of what had happened and asked her to make some coffee to warm them up. There were still some embers left in the brazier, covered with ashes so that Loke could use them to start the fire up again in the morning. But the embers weren't enough to warm their shivering limbs.

Mark-Alem lost no time going up to bed; but he couldn't get to sleep.

When he got up at daybreak he found his mother and Loke just where he'd left them, huddled around the almost dead coals.

"Where are you going, Mark?" said his mother in a terrified voice.

"To the office," he answered. "Where do you think?"

"Are you out of your mind? On a day like this!"

She and Loke both tried to persuade him not to go that day—just that day—to his wretched work; to say he wasn't well; to give some more serious reason for his absence; but at all costs to stay away. But he wouldn't be persuaded. They both implored him again, especially his mother, kissing his hands and bathing them in tears, and saying that on such a day the Tabir Sarrail might not even be open. But the more she begged, the more he insisted on going. Finally he managed to tear himself away and leave the house.

Outside it was more than usually cold. He walked briskly along the street, which as usual at this hour was almost empty. The few passersby, their faces muffled up in shawls, still looked drowsy. His own head was no clearer than theirs. He still hadn't got over the scene of the night before. Just as certain marine creatures secrete a protective cloud around them, so his brain seemed to have invented a way of avoiding lucid thought. Sometimes he even wondered if anything had really happened at all. It might just have been one of those wild imaginings that filled so many files in the Tabir Sarrail. But the truth finally pierced his brain like a needle, after which his mind fell back into a daze, followed by a lull, which in turn was followed by the shooting pain once more. He'd noticed that in attacks of this kind, the awakening after the first night was particularly disagreeable. He felt as if he were in some fluid intermediate state between sleeping and waking. And his own state seemed to be reflected in the world around him—in the walls of the buildings patched with damp, and the ashen faces of the passersby. These grew more numerous as he approached the middle of the town. He could tell by the way they hurried along—perhaps it had something to do with the fact that they all had the same office hours—which were the ones who worked in ministries and other government offices.

And when he got to the Palace of the Sheikh-ul-Islam he saw there were more soldiers of the Guard on duty than the day before. Their helmets, wet with dew, glinted dully. There were soldiers posted at the crossroads by the bank. Apparently the state of emergency hadn't been lifted. No, none of this was an illusion. And Kurt was in prison. Perhaps even . . . The bloodstained carpet that the footmen had rolled up kept enveloping his own thoughts. How would he ever be able to set foot on a carpet again without feeling faint? He felt the desire to vomit rising again. . . .

So the Palace of Dreams is open, he said to himself when he saw the entrances from a distance. The employees were flocking around the doors. Most of them didn't know one another and didn't greet, let alone talk to, their colleagues. But in the corridor by the Interpretation Department Mark-Alem did see some familiar faces. And luckily his neighbor was already sitting at his desk.

"So," he said as soon as Mark-Alem had sat down beside him. "Have you found out anything?"

"No, I don't know a thing," lied Mark-Alem. "I've only just arrived. What's happened?"

"I don't know anything definite myself, but it's obvious something important has been going on. Did you see the soldiers in the street?"

"Yes—last night and today."

The other, while pretending to be busy with his file, leaned nearer to Mark-Alem and whispered:

"It seems something has happened to the Quprilis, but no one knows what exactly."

Mark-Alem felt his heartbeats slacken.

Idiot, he said to himself. You know all about it, so why do you let yourself be affected by what anyone else says?

Nevertheless he asked:

"What do you mean?"

His voice had grown faint, as if he feared that to hear what had happened might make it real.

"I don't know anything definite. It's only a rumor, perhaps mere gossip."

"Maybe," said Mark-Alem, bending over his file and saying to himself, You silly idiot—do you think it's all going to be sorted out as easily as that?

His eyes were incapable of taking anything in. There in front of him was a senseless dream that he was supposed to explain, while he was ten times more crazy himself. The other clerks were all poring over their files. Every so often you could hear the rustle of pages being turned.

"Even today you can feel a kind of uneasiness everywhere,'' muttered his neighbor. "Something's bound to happen."

What else *can* happen? thought Mark-Alem. His head felt as heavy as lead. It seemed to him he might easily fall asleep over his open file and drop a dream on it, like a hen laying an egg. What nonsense, he thought, rubbing his brow. My mind must be wandering. Perhaps after all I'd have done better to stay at home.

Never before had he looked forward so eagerly to the bell for break. His eyes were half closed over the sleep of someone else, as described in the file. Before long his own sleep would merge with the other, as sometimes two human destinies blindly join.

The bell for break startled him. He slowly followed the others down to the basement. The usual hubbub reigned there, as if nothing had happened. Of course, for the others nothing *had* happened. He tried to catch bits of the conversations going on around him, but none of them had anything to do with what had occurred. Anyway, he thought, what's the point? No one knew as much as he did about what had taken place. He couldn't learn anything from their senseless comments.

He had a coffee and started slowly up the stairs again. Beside him the others went on chatting about this and that. Two or three times he thought he caught the word "siege," and people asking, "Did you see the sentries last night?" But he walked on, asking himself what concern it was of his.

He really thought he didn't want to find out anything, even out of curiosity. But when he sat down at his desk he realized he was eagerly awaiting his neighbor's return.

Finally he appeared in the doorway. Mark-Alem could tell by the way he walked that he had news.

"Apparently it's a dream that's behind it all," the other

man whispered as soon as he got near enough.

"All what?"

"What do you mean, what? Behind the disgrace that's fallen upon the Quprilis."

"Oh! So it's true?"

"Yes, it's been confirmed. They've been hit very hard. I suspected as much! People had a presentiment here yesterday evening. . . ."

"What sort of dream was it?"

"A strange one, dreamed by a street merchant. You always think that at first—you believe it's about innocent things like vegetables or grassy plains, and then you find out there's some great disaster behind it all. It was that kind of dream, with a bridge and a flute, or a violin—some kind of musical instrument, anyway."

"A bridge and a musical instrument?" gasped Mark-Alem all in one breath. "And then what? What else was there?"

"Some animal going around in circles—but the main thing was the bridge, and the violin."

Mark-Alem felt as if an elephant were treading on his chest. He'd held the wretched dream in his hands, twice.

"What's the matter? You don't look well. . . ."

"It's nothing. I felt rather off-color yesterday evening, and I was vomiting all night."

"You look like it. But what was I talking about?"

"The dream."

"Oh yes . . . So it was the dream that acted as a clue. They deciphered its meaning, and everything was clear. The bridge stood for the Quprilis, you see—*Qupri* means bridge. And after that the whole thing unraveled of its own accord."

So that's what it was! Mark-Alem felt his mouth go dry. He remembered now how he had tried in vain to find a link between the bridge and the raging bull, which certainly symbolized destructive force, and how he had put the dream in the file of those that remained undeciphered.

Now that someone else had elucidated it—and so successfully!—perhaps he would be asked to explain why he had failed to do so? Perhaps he'd be suspected of setting it aside deliberately in order to cover things up. What could be more natural, seeing he himself was a Quprili? True, he could defend himself by saying that as he was working in Selection at the time, he could have eliminated the dream altogether if he'd wanted to, whereas in fact he'd sent it on to Interpretation. But he couldn't help feeling that such excuses were likely to fall on deaf ears.

"And then," his neighbor went on, "the violin, or whatever it was, was connected to an epic they sing about the Quprilis in the Balkans. But hey, what's up with you now? Are you feeling ill?"

He nodded, unable to speak. To avoid arousing suspicion rather than because he really wanted to listen, he signed to the other to go on. Now that his neighbor had mentioned the epic, he lost all hope that this trouble might be the product of an unruly imagination. Kurt's arrest and the murder of the rhapsodists were further reasons for thinking the epic had something to do with what had happened, and that the dream was at the root of it all. The meaning of the dream now seemed as clear as day: The Quprilis (the bridge), through their epic (the musical instrument), were engaged in some action against the State (the angry bull). Why hadn't he seen it earlier? It had been in his power to avert the disaster, and he had done nothing. There had been nothing accidental about that dinner with the Vizier, or about his uncle's vague warnings and exhortations to be on the alert. But he had been incapable of seeing the clue, he had gone to sleep over his files, and misfortune had descended on his nearest and dearest.

"Do you feel a bit better now?" asked his colleague.

"Yes, a bit."

"Good. Don't worry—it'll pass. As I was saying, the epic was apparently the cause of friction between the Quprilis and the Sovereign in the old days. The family's supporters have been urging them for a long time to renounce it, but apparently they've always refused, although they've often had to suffer for it. And there's something else; as if the Slav epic wasn't enough, they invited some Albanian rhapsodists to come and perform *their* version! I ask you! They were digging their own graves. That was what really made the Sovereign fly off the handle. He decided to put a stop to the business once and for all—to root out the confounded epic altogether. It seems a group of officials is even being organized to rush to the Balkans and eliminate the Albanian epic, which is regarded as the cause of the whole trouble."

"Really? Really?" Mark-Alem kept interjecting. He was really thinking, How on earth does he know all this?

"Feeling better now?" said the other again. "I told you it'd pass. Where was I? Oh yes—on top of all the rest they expect this to bring about a deterioration in relations with Austria and a rapprochement with Russia. The Russian ambassador could scarcely conceal his satisfaction at the reception last night."

Mark-Alem remembered the terror in the face of the Austrian consul's son the previous evening. God, it must all be true! he thought. But he said to his neighbor:

"But what's Russia got to do with those wretched epics?"

"Russia? I wondered that too, but things are a little more complicated than they look, my lad. This is not just a matter of poetry and song, as it might appear at first blush. If it was only that, our great Sovereign wouldn't deign to bother with it. But in fact it's an exceedingly complex business, to do with settlements and transfers of population in the Balkans, and the relations between Slav peoples and non-Slav peoples, like the Albanians. In short, it directly concerns the whole map of the Balkans. For this epic, as I said, is sung in two languages, Albanian and Slav, and is connected with questions of ethnic frontiers inside the Empire. I too wondered at first what Austria, not to mention Russia, had to do with it. But it seems both of them are involved. Austria supports the non-Slav peoples, whereas the Slavs' 'little father,' the Tsar, is always on at our Sultan about the way the people of his race are treated. He has informers everywhere. And this epic deals precisely with the relations between the peoples of the Balkans. Apparently the Albanese rhapsodists were murdered at the Quprili house, and their instruments smashed with them. Do you still feel ill?''

Mark-Alem blinked.

"Never mind, it'll pass. I've suffered from the same thing myself. Yes, old boy, things are always more complicated than they seem. Those of us who work here think we're well informed, but in reality all that we know amounts to a handful of dreams, a few clouds. . . .''

He droned on for a while, his voice getting lower and lower until in the end he was mumbling more or less to himself. Mark-Alem's brain felt ground to bits by what he'd just heard. If only he'd destroyed the dream in Selection, while he had it in his power—nipped it in the bud as one crushes the head of a young viper to stop it from growing up and doing mischief! But he'd let it escape, let it glide from file to file, from section to section, growing and accumulating venom until at last it turned into a Master-Dream. He suffered pangs of remorse. Every so often he would try to console himself: Perhaps the dream would have made its way to its goal whatever happened, since it was in the interests of such powerful factions, even whole states, that it should do so. And even if he had destroyed it, mightn't means have been found to fabricate another? Hadn't the Vizier given him clearly to understand that dreams *were* fabricated, even Master-Dreams? No, he'd been right, absolutely right not to get mixed up in it. Otherwise there might have been an inquiry afterward, they might have found out that he'd suppressed that bit of evidence, and then the punishment (which he was afraid of incurring anyway for not having deciphered the dream) would have been terrible, and fallen not only on him but also on all his family. Perhaps that was why the Vizier hadn't given him precise instructions about what to do. And if his uncle had hesitated, perhaps it was because he himself didn't know what was the best course to follow. Oh, groaned Mark-Alem inwardly, why did I ever set foot in this cursed place?

"We're expecting the official eulogy today," he heard his neighbor's voice say.

"Eulogy? What for?"

"What for? Because of the dream, of course—the dream is at the root of everything. You *are* in the clouds. What have we been talking about all this time?"

"Of course . . . Whatever am I thinking of?"

"Oh well, you've got an excuse—you're not feeling well. Yes, the people in Selection were congratulated this morning. And the other sections, starting with Reception, have probably been commended. Perhaps the official eulogy, and the reward that goes with it, has already been sent to the greengrocer. . . . But what I can't understand is why Interpretation hasn't received any congratulations yet."

"Hasn't it?"

"I haven't mentioned it before, but there's a feeling of nervousness in this section this morning. And perhaps that's the reason: The congratulations haven't arrived."

"Why not?"

"Who knows? I've been watching the boss; he's looking worried. Don't you agree?"

"Yes."

"He's got reason to worry. Interpretation deserves congratulations more than anyone. Unless . . ."

"Unless what?"

"Unless its interpretation had turned out to be wrong."

"But in that case, how would it have been corrected? There's no other section that deals with deciphering after Interpretation. The Master-Dream officials deal only with the choice of dreams, don't they?"

"Yes," said the other, somewhat surprised to see Mark-Alem reviving slightly. "It's hard to puzzle it out. But we still don't know why the congratulations are late. . . ."

They both plunged back briefly into their files. But neither could read the lines in front of them. What if he knows about my connection with the Quprilis? thought Mark-Alem. But he'd find out about it sooner or later anyway. And the boss must know already, even if he was for the moment concealing the fact that the Quprilis' downfall was the event of the day. But perhaps the boss had troubles of his own? Come what might, Mark-Alem was sure everyone would soon be looking askance at him, if he wasn't simply dismissed outright.

"They've just sent for the boss again," whispered his neighbor. "He's as white as a sheet; have you noticed?"

"Yes, yes . . ."

"I told you—this delay's a bad sign. It's clear there won't be any congratulations now. Let's hope there aren't any . . ."

"Any what?" asked Mark-Alem in a choked voice.

"Punishments."

"But why . . . why should there be any punishments?"

He felt a faint stirring of hope revive deep down inside him. But his face was ashen, and he looked as if he might faint.

"How should I know?" answered the other. "It's completely beyond me."

The fellow was getting more and more edgy. The idea that something was going on that he didn't know about was more than he could bear. He kept looking impatiently either at the inner door, or at the one through which their boss had disappeared, or at the one that opened on to the corridor.

"There's something going on. . . ." he muttered. "No doubt about it. It's awful, awful. . . ."

He was showing his exasperation quite openly now, but it was impossible to tell whether what was awful was what was happening or the fact that he couldn't find out anything about it.

Mark-Alem had never wished so fervently that his neighbor's words might be true. He who until now had shuddered at the news that something was going on now prayed with all his heart that something really might be happening. If the congratulations for the wretched dream still hadn't arrived, and they really were expecting to be reprimanded, this might mean the situation had been reversed at the last minute. . . . Out of superstition he dismissed such optimistic conjectures, in case merely thinking of them prevented them from coming true. It certainly would be a miracle. . . .

"It's as plain as a pikestaff—you'd have to be blind not to see it. . . ." his neighbor hissed angrily, as if it were Mark-Alem who was preventing his theories from proving correct.

Here and there at their desks the clerks were whispering among themselves. Those who were near the windows craned

their necks to see outside. Apparently repercussions of what
was going on had managed to reach as far as there.

Mark-Alem thought of the carriages with the letter Q on
them driving about wildly through the darkness, and for the
first time he was really sure something further must have
happened since last night. The Vizier wouldn't have just stood
there doing nothing. The way he had controlled his fury when
he left the fatal room; the way he had gone upstairs like a
sleepwalker—all this suggested he might hit back. And what
about the carriage that had driven off into the night, and
those his mother and he had seen in the darkness without
knowing where they were going to or where they were
coming from . . . ? God, if only it was true!

"I can't stand it any longer," said his neighbor. "I'm off
to find out what's what. If anyone asks for me, say I've gone
down to the Archives."

He slipped out as quietly as a shadow. As he watched him,
Mark-Alem felt a surge of relief. At least he was going to find
out something now.

He sat for some time staring at his file, unable to make out
a word. He was anxious to hear the latest news, but if his
neighbor didn't come back at once, it must be because he was
collecting lots of information. But Mark-Alem made superhu-
man efforts to stifle unfounded hopes. He knew that another
disappointment would finish him off.

Now not only those near the windows kept looking out,
but—and this had never happened before—other clerks from
nearby tables crowded around to look out, too. There was no
denying it; something out of the ordinary was in the air.
Mark-Alem looked alternately at the windows, and at the
door through which he expected his neighbor to reappear.
Could the Sovereign have sent back the Master-Dream as if it
were a young bride who turned out not to be a virgin?

He didn't want to be too hopeful, but what was happening now was simply inconceivable. All the clerks, not only those in the middle of the room but also those on the far side, were crowding around the windows. He saw people get up and go over to look out who had never stirred from their places before, who had seemed to be riveted to their desks, and who not only had never dreamed of going and looking out of the windows, but had probably never even realized that the room they worked in actually *had* windows.

Mark-Alem was consumed with impatience. He waited and waited, and then did what an hour before would have struck him as ridiculous. He crossed the room and joined the others at one of the windows.

His heart couldn't have beaten faster if he'd been standing on the brink of an abyss. As a matter of fact, that was what the darkness outside suggested. Various clerks leaned on the window ledges, peering out.

"What's happening?" whispered Mark-Alem.

Someone turned around and looked at him in amazement.

"Can't you see what's going on down in the courtyard?"

Mark-Alem looked where the other was looking. For the first time he realized that these windows looked out on one of the inner courtyards of the Palace of Dreams. The courtyard was swarming with soldiers. From above they looked foreshortened and thin, but their helmets glinted dangerously.

"I can see some soldiers," said Mark-Alem.

The other didn't answer.

"But what are they there for?" asked Mark-Alem.

But the other had disappeared.

Mark-Alem glanced down again at the armed men, who looked as if they were made of lead. He was dazed, and thought confusedly of the carriages with the letter Q carved on the doors, which for some reason always made him think of night birds. Because of this confusion he found himself thinking of them sometimes as vehicles and sometimes as owls winging through the dark.

"What's the matter?" said a voice nearby, in a brief respite between asthmatic wheezings.

"Can't you see—down in the courtyard?" Mark-Alem answered.

The other man's breath was making the icy windowpanes mist over. Mark-Alem's mind seemed to drift away for a moment; then the cold cleared the glass again, and Mark-Alem's thoughts too. He went slowly back to his desk. His neighbor had returned.

"Where've you been?" he asked Mark-Alem. "I've been waiting ages for you."

Mark-Alem nodded toward the window.

"Nonsense! How can you find anything out from up here? But wait till you hear *my* news. Sensational! They say some of the staff of Interpretation are going to be arrested. Starting with the head of the section."

Mark-Alem swallowed painfully.

"The courtyard's swarming with soldiers," he muttered.

"Yes, but they're there for something else. It seems that even some of the high-ups in the Tabir are going to be arrested."

"My God—what can it mean?"

"The Quprilis have struck back. It was only to be expected."

"Struck back?" stammered Mark-Allen. "Who? How? Against whom?"

"Hold on—don't be in such a hurry! I'm just going to explain. Only come a bit closer—we don't want to end up like them! . . . The whole of the Tabir Sarrail is in a turmoil.

Last night, or early this morning rather, something very strange happened . . .''

The carriages that seemed like owls . . . thought Mark-Alem. He also remembered there was a bird, the eagle owl, known as the grand duke. . . .

"After the blow fell on them, the Quprilis didn't just sit idly by. They acted at once, during the night, and in some way neither you nor I nor anyone else can guess at, at least for the moment. It was apparently at dawn that they managed to carry out their plan. But as I say, it's still all shrouded in mystery. Some confrontation, some secret and terrible exchange of blows has taken place in the darkest depths of the State. We've felt only the surface repercussions, as you do in an earthquake with a very deep hypocenter. . . . So, as I was saying, during the night a terrible clash took place between the two rival groups, the two forces that counterbalance one another within the State. The entire capital is in an uproar, but no one knows anything definite. After all, even we, who're at the very source of the mystery, are still in the dark.''

Mark-Alem was tempted to say he had handled the beastly dream twice himself, but a moment's reflection was enough to remind him that this would be folly.

"Even before daybreak,'' his neighbor prattled on, "carriages were seen coming and going between the embassies and the Foreign Ministry. But that's not all. Apparently the Empire's leading banks and the big copper mines are implicated too. There's even talk of devaluation.''

"Good gracious!'' exclaimed Mark-Alem.

"So that's how things are. Very confused, and very different from what they appear. As if they were taking place down a bottomless pit . . . And as I said, all we have to guide us is a handful of dreams, a few scraps of cloud. . . .''

* * *

All *that day* the Palace of Dreams was racked by deep anxiety. Early in the afternoon the head of Interpretation and a number of the Tabir's other senior officials were indeed arrested. Other arrests were expected to follow immediately. But evening came without any further developments.

Mark-Alem went home, eager to tell his mother all he knew. He was surprised that she didn't look more delighted.

They sent someone to the Vizier's house, hoping he might bring back some good news about Kurt, but the messenger returned saying no one knew anything about him.

Although he'd had very little rest the previous night, Mark-Alem couldn't sleep a wink. At one point he thought he was about to drop off, but a noise in the distance brought him wide awake. He got up and went to the window, but couldn't see anything. Then he noticed a faint red glow on the horizon, and he thought in a flash, What if the Palace of Dreams is on fire? But he soon realized the fire lay in a completely different direction. Back in bed, he tossed and turned for a long time before falling asleep. He woke before dawn, got up straightaway, shaved carefully, and prepared, much earlier than usual, to set off for the Tabir Sarrail.

THE COMING
OF SPRING

vii.

...

N o   o n e   w a s e v e r   t o   k n o w

what really happened that night. As the days went by,

the fog that had enveloped not only the details but also

the very nature of the event, instead of dispersing, only

grew denser.

The arrests in the Palace of Dreams went on for a

whole week. The brunt of the blow fell on the Master-

Dream officers. Those who escaped prison were trans-

ferred to Selection or Reception or even to the copyists'

department. Conversely, some of the staff in Selection

and Interpretation were sent to fill the spaces left in the Master-Dream section. Mark-Alem was among the first to be moved in this way. Two days later, before he had got over the excitement of the move, he was sent for by head office, which had been decimated by the arrests, and the Director-General in person told him he was being made head of the Master-Dream section.

He was staggered. Such a huge leap forward in his career was almost unthinkable. The Quprilis were obviously getting their own back.

Meanwhile, there was no news of Kurt. The Vizier was always busy. Mark-Alem couldn't understand why his uncle, when he'd been powerful enough to shake the foundations of the State, couldn't manage to get his own brother out of prison. But perhaps he had his own reasons for taking his time. Or perhaps he thought things were best left as they were.

Mark-Alem himself was overwhelmed with work and hadn't time to indulge in long reflections. The section had to be reorganized from top to bottom. Unexamined files were piling up. And it would soon be Friday, the day when the Master-Dream was sent to the Sovereign.

Mark-Alem's mood had grown even more somber than before, and he was becoming increasingly unapproachable. Despite his efforts to remain his old self, he could feel that something was gradually changing, in what he said, what he did, even in the way he worked. He identified more and more with the sort of people he'd always liked least: the senior civil servants.

As the days went by he grew more and more conscious of the importance of his new post. He now had a sky-blue carriage at his disposal, waiting for him outside the Palace, and he felt it was not merely this equipage but he himself who commanded respect, silence, and fear. He was tempted to smile at this, finding it almost incredible that he, recently so fearful about the mystery of the State and the oppressive atmosphere emanating from its organs, should now cause the same apprehension in others. But he sometimes thought that was only in the nature of things. It was probably because he was so sensitive, building up so much mystery and anguish inside himself, that he now spread the overflow around him.

He was so taken up with his work he didn't notice that the weather was growing milder. Although, after the murder of the rhapsodists, all Albania had fallen prey to insomnia, the Palace machine was working flat out. As one of the most senior officials, Mark-Alem received the ultra-secret detail report every morning. The amount of sleep registered in the various regions varied in accordance with the events that took place there. A special report had been called for on the subject of Albania's insomnia. The street trader who'd sent in the fateful dream had been in solitary confinement for several days. They were still trying to get the explanations they needed out of him, and the record of his depositions had already filled four hundred pages. In general, a period of disturbed sleep was expected, with a steep rise in the wilder kind of dream. Mark-Alem had got into the habit, in moments of weariness, of rubbing his eyes at length, as if to remove the veil drawn over them by so much reading.

One evening when he got home as usual, he found Loke looking very pale. Again he felt in his midriff the familiar hollow of anxiety, almost forgotten in the last few weeks.

"What's the matter?" he breathed. "Is it Kurt?"

Loke nodded.

"Isn't he going to be freed? How many years' imprisonment has he been sentenced to?"

Loke's eyes, almost dissolving in tears, just gazed at him sadly.

"I asked you how long a sentence they've given him," Mark-Alem repeated. But still she didn't answer. Just went on gazing at him tearfully.

He grabbed her by the shoulders and shook her, then, gradually guessing what had happened, burst into tears himself.

Kurt had been sentenced to death and decapitated. The news had just arrived.

Mark-Alem went and shut himself up in his room, while his mother wept alone in hers. How could it have happened? he kept asking himself. How could it be that, when Kurt's release had seemed just a matter of days, he could have been condemned to death and summarily executed? He clutched his brow. Did this mean that the Quprilis' counterattack, their recovery of power and his own meteoric rise, were only illusions, a false triumph preceding some new blow? But he didn't care about anything anymore. Let them strike, the sooner and the more cruelly the better, and get the whole business over once and for all.

Next morning, pale and wan, he went into the Tabir Sarrail, convinced he was going to be relieved of his new post and sent back to his former duties in Interpretation, or even in Selection. But his subordinates greeted him with the same respect as they had always shown since his promotion, and his pallor seemed to make them even more attentive. As they came and set various papers in front of him, he examined their expressions and their words for signs of mockery. Finding none, he felt reassured. But this didn't last long. His anxiety revived at the thought that even if his dismissal or demotion had already been decided, his staff wouldn't know about it yet. He thought up an excuse for going to see the Director-General, and when he was told the Director-General was unwell and not coming in that day, this merely seemed part of the elaborate joke that was being played on him.

Mark-Alem's anxiety lasted several days. Then early one morning—he'd noticed that everything that happened to him did so when he least expected it—the Director-General sent for him. About time too! thought Mark-Alem as he got up to go. Strangely enough, he didn't feel any emotion. It was as if he'd gone deaf and the only sound was that of his footsteps as he went along the corridor. When he presented himself in the Director-General's office, he was struck by the extreme gravity of the other's expression. Of course, he thought, it's only natural he should be serious when it's a question of dismissing a Quprili. In their family, both promotion and its opposite were always dealt with ceremoniously. The Director was talking to him, but he wasn't listening. He wasn't really interested in what he had to say. He just wanted to get out of this office as fast as possible and go to the section he was being sent to, whether it was Selection or even copying, and there take an unassuming place amid the hundreds of anonymous clerks. At one point he felt inclined to interrupt: Why not cut it short? What was the point of beating about the bush? There was no point in these long preambles. But apparently the Director enjoyed playing cat and mouse with him. Who knows, perhaps he wasn't sorry to be getting rid of this young sprig from the Quprili family. Perhaps it had even occurred to him that he, Mark-Alem, might one day do him out of his job. As a matter of fact he'd once hinted at the possibility. . . .

Mark-Alem frowned. How dared the man use such coarse sarcasm on him? It was going too far! Now the Director was actually offering him his congratulations! Easy for him to make fun of me! he thought. And then a moment later: I must be going crazy. . . .

"Mark-Alem—don't you feel well?" said the Director solicitously.

"Go on—I'm listening," he answered coldly.

Now it was the Director's turn to be astonished. He smiled tentatively.

"I must admit I didn't expect you to react like this. . . ."

"What do you mean?" said Mark-Alem as curtly as before.

The Director-General flung out his arms.

"Of course, everyone has the right to receive news like this as he thinks fit. All the more so in the case of someone like you, coming from an illustrious family of prime ministers . . ."

"I'd be obliged if you'd get to the point," said Mark-Alem, who could feel the perspiration trickling down his forehead.

The Director-General stared.

"I thought I'd made myself perfectly clear," he muttered. "To tell the truth, I still can't take it in myself . . . calling someone to my office to tell them that . . ."

Mark-Alem could scarcely hear for the buzzing in his ears. What the other was saying was simply incredible. Gradually, bit by bit, it penetrated to his brain. The words "appointment," "dismissal," "replacing the Director-General," "post of Director-General" really had been uttered, but with a completely different meaning from what he had at first supposed. For a good quarter of an hour the Director-General of the Tabir Sarrail had been explaining that he, Mark-Alem, while continuing in his post as head of the Master-Dream section, was also, by direct orders from on high, appointed First Assistant Director of the Palace of Dreams, and thus assistant to himself, the Director-General, who, as Mark-Alem knew, would often be absent for reasons of health.

The Director-General, as he slowly repeated what he had already said once, seemed to be trying to make out why this news should have met with such a cool reception. But his amazement was now accompanied by a tinge of suspicion.

Mark-Alem rubbed his eyes, then without lowering his hands murmured:

"I'm sorry. I'm not feeling very well today. Please forgive me."

"No, no . . . don't worry about it," said the Director. "As a matter of fact, I could tell you were unwell as soon as you came in. You must take better care of yourself, especially now that you're going to have all this extra work. I wasn't careful enough myself, and now, as you see, I'm paying the price. Anyway, let me congratulate you! With all my heart! Good luck!"

Every time he recalled this tête-à-tête in the days that followed, Mark-Alem felt an almost physical pain. On top of that, he was overwhelmed with work. The Director-General was absent most of the time for health reasons, and Mark-Alem had to replace him for several days running. Burdened as he was, he'd become even more morose. The gigantic mechanism, which he was now to all intents and purposes running, functioned day and night. Only now did he realize how vast the Tabir Sarrail really was. Senior State officials were timid when they entered his office. The Assistant Minister of the Interior, who visited him often, was careful never to interrupt him when he spoke. In the Assistant Minister's eyes, as in those of all the other senior officials, there was, despite their polite smiles, a constant query: Is there a dream about me? . . . Being powerful and laden with honors, holding important posts and enjoying influential support—all this was not enough to reassure them. What mattered was not merely what they were in life; equally important was the part they played in other people's dreams, the mysterious carriages they drove in in those dreams, and the emblems and cabalistic signs carved on their carriage doors. . . .

Every morning, when the daily report was brought in to him, Mark-Alem felt as if he were holding in his hands the previous night of millions and millions of people. Anyone who ruled over the dark zones of men's lives wielded enormous power. And with every week that went by, Mark-Alem grew more aware of this.

One day, on a sudden impulse, he got up from his desk and went slowly down to the Archives. There he met with the same oppressive smell of coal as before. The clerks stood there in front of him, self-effacing, like shadows, ready to do his bidding. He asked for the file containing the Master-Dreams for the last few months. When it was brought, he told the staff to leave him to work in peace, and began to leaf steadily through the pages. His trembling fingers showed his growing tension. His heartbeats slackened. At the top of each page, on the right, was written, among various other details, the date of the dream it recorded. Last Friday in December. First Friday in January. Second Friday in January. And here at last was the dream he was looking for, the fateful Master-Dream that had led his uncle to the grave and raised him, Mark-Alem, to be a director of the Tabir. He found it difficult to read the dream; it was as if there were a white bandage over his eyes that let in only thin shafts of light.

It really was the dream of the greengrocer who had a stall in the capital—the dream he'd held in his hand twice before—together with the rough interpretation which he already knew: the bridge, from the word *Qupri,* meaning Quprili; the musical instrument, signifying the Albanian epic;

the red bull which, maddened by the music, would rush upon the State. My God! he breathed. It had all been engraved on his mind before, but seeing it here in black and white made him tremble from head to foot. He closed the file and walked slowly away.

Since he'd been appointed to the head of the Tabir Sarrail, he'd learned a great many terrifying secrets, but until now he'd never succeeded in clearing up the mystery of that night, with the attack on the Quprilis followed by their counter-attack.

The greengrocer was still being interrogated in his cell. The record of his depositions now covered more than eight hundred pages, and still there was no sign that it was going to be brought to an end. One day Mark-Alem sent for the file and spent several hours studying it. It was the first time he'd ever seen such a document. The hundreds of pages were full of minute details about the greengrocer's daily life. Everything was included, or almost everything: the kinds of fruit and vegetables he sold—cabbages, cauliflowers, peppers, lettuces; the times when they were delivered; how they were unloaded; how fresh the various items were; quarrels with suppliers; fluctuations in prices; customers and what they said, and how it reflected family problems, economic difficulties, hidden illnesses, conflicts, crises, alliances; scraps of overheard gossip; things that drunks, road-sweepers and idlers said as night fell; the sayings of unknown passersby which for some reason or other had remained in his memory; and again all the vegetables and what they tasted like at the beginning and at the end of the season; how they were moistened to make them seem fresh; the doltishness of the peasants who brought them in; haggling over prices; the throw-outs; how dew made lettuces weigh more; the whims and fancies of housewives; the squabbles; the rows—and all of these things gone over and over interminably.

When he'd shut the bulky file, Mark-Alem felt as if he were emerging from a vast meadow damp with dew, an innocent field which you'd never have dreamed could have harbored a viper. Although reading the file had tired him, he felt in a way refreshed, and was surprised to find he was inclined to pity the greengrocer, who seemed not to have the slightest idea of the consequences of his dream. But before Mark-Alem went on to read the explanation of the dream, which probably took up hundreds more pages, he had to consider whether the greengrocer really had dreamed the dream in question. But after all, that didn't matter now; things had taken their course, and there was no going back.

In the days that followed, Mark-Alem stopped thinking about the greengrocer. Spring was on the way, probably bringing all kinds of tension to the Palace of Dreams, and he wouldn't have time for trivialities. All the reports that were brought to him bristled with problems. Albania's insomnia continued; such a thing had never been seen before. Admittedly it wasn't up to the Palace of Dreams to set these matters right, yet as long as the tension lasted, the Tabir had to keep very careful records of the increasing sleeplessness. To crown all, the Director of the Imperial Bank, in the course of a long interview he'd had with Mark-Alem a few days before, had mentioned the possibility of devaluation as the probable result of the serious economic crisis the Empire was going through. So it was up to the Palace of Dreams to take note of this state of affairs and pay extra-careful attention to dreams on this subject. Mark-Alem knew, from his brief experience in Selection and Interpretation, that there were always hundreds of such dreams in the files.

Other important State institutions, more indirectly, called his attention to the unrest currently prevailing in Jewish and

Armenian intellectual circles (God, were they asking for some new massacre?) and to a certain slackening of the links between the major pashaliks and the metropolis. Probably for the umpteenth time, these institutions renewed their warnings against the weakening of religious feeling among the younger generation. It was well known that such warnings derived from the Sheikh-ul-Islam.

Mark-Alem, absorbed by all these preoccupations, was unaware of the approach of spring. The weather was slightly warmer, the migrating storks had returned, but he didn't notice.

One afternoon, at the same time and almost at the same place in the corridor as before, he saw some men silently carrying a coffin out of one of the cells. The greengrocer, he said to himself, without looking after them to make sure or to find out more. A little while later, as he was being jolted along in his carriage, the sight of the little procession came back to him. But he drove it away. Outside, in the crimson light of the setting sun, he could see the first shoots of grass in the gardens of the houses, though the trees were still bare.

At home he found his eldest uncle, the governor, and his wife, together with some other close relations. The governor hadn't been back to the capital since Kurt's execution. They were all talking about Mark-Alem's betrothal. His mother's eyes were damp, as if spring had reached her at least. He listened absently to what they were saying, without contributing to the conversation himself. With some surprise, as if at some sudden revelation, he realized he was twenty-eight years old. Since he'd started working in the Palace of Dreams, where time obeyed completely different laws, he'd practically never given a thought to his age.

Encouraged by his silence, the others started to speak more confidently about the girl they had in mind for him. She was nineteen, and fair—he liked blondes. They led the conversation around to the subject very carefully, as if they were holding a crystal goblet in their hands. Mark-Alem didn't say either yes or no. And in the days that followed, as if to avoid jeopardizing what they thought was their success, they refrained from mentioning the matter further.

At home, apart from the two dinner parties that his mother held in honor of her eldest brother, that week was uneventful. The sculptor usually employed to see to the family's graves came to submit suggestions for the inscription on Kurt's tombstone and the bronze ornaments to be added to it.

The following week Mark-Alem got home late every evening. He had more work than he could cope with. The Sovereign had asked for a long report on the sleep and dreams of the whole Empire. People were working overtime in every section of the Tabir Sarrail. The Director-General was still unwell, and Mark-Alem had to write the final version of the report.

Every so often as he sat at his desk, he would feel his head grow heavy, and wonder at the pages already written as if it had been someone else who'd penned them. There before him lay the melancholy aggregate of the sleep of one of the vastest empires in the world: more than forty nationalities, representatives of almost all religions and of every race. If the report had included the whole globe, it wouldn't have made much difference. To all intents and purposes it covered the sleep of the entire planet—terrible and infinite shadows, a bottomless abyss from which Mark-Alem was trying to dredge up a few fragments of truth. Hypnos himself, the Greek god of sleep, couldn't have known more than he did about dreams.

One afternoon he got his family's *Chronicle* out of the library. The last time he'd looked at it was that cold morning

when, newly appointed, he was about to present himself for
the first time at the Palace of which he was now virtually the
Director. As he turned the pages he still wasn't sure what he
was looking for. Then he realized he wasn't looking for
anything. All he wanted was to get to the blank pages at the
end. . . . It was the first time it had ever occurred to him to
add something to this ancient chronicle. For a long while he
sat still, gazing at the ledger. Important things had been
happening. The war against Russia was just over. Greece had
left the Empire, and the rest of the Balkans was in turmoil.
As for Albania . . . It grew more and more distant and dim,
like some far cold constellation, and he wondered if he really
knew anything about what went on there. . . . He sat there
uncertainly, his pen growing heavy in his hand, until finally it
rested on the paper and instead of writing "Albania" wrote:
There. He gazed at the expression that had substituted itself
for the name of his homeland, and suddenly felt oppressed by
what he immediately thought of as "Quprilian sadness." It
was a term unknown to any other language in the world,
though it ought to be incorporated in them all.

   It must have been snowing . . . there. . . . Then he
stopped writing, snatching away the pen as if afraid it might
be held to the paper by magic. It was with an effort that he
went on to record, in the succinct style used in the rest of the
Chronicle, the death of Kurt and his own appointment as
head of the Palace of Dreams. Then his pen was still again, and
he thought of the distant ancestor called Gjon who on a
winter's day several centuries before had built a bridge and at
the same time edified his name. The patronymic bore within
it, like a secret message, the destiny of the Quprilis for
generation after generation. And so that the bridge might
endure, a man was sacrificed in its building, walled up in its
foundations. And although so much time had gone by since,

the traces of his blood had come down to the present generation. So that the Quprilis might endure . . .

Perhaps that was why—like the ancient Greeks, cutting off
their hair at a funeral so that the angry soul of the departed
wouldn't be able to recognize them and do them harm—
perhaps that was why the Quprilis had changed their name to
Köprülü: to avoid being identified with the bridge.

Mark-Alem knew all about this, but remembered how on
the fateful night he had longed to throw off the protective
mask, the Islamic half-shield of "Alem," and adopt one of
those ancient names that attracted danger and were marked
by fate.

As before he repeated to himself: Mark-Gjergj Ura, Mark-
Gjorg Ura . . . still holding the pen poised in his hand, as if
uncertain what name to append to the ancient chronicle. . . .

Late one afternoon in March he finished the report, and sent
it to the copyists' office to be transcribed. Then, with some
relief, he went out to his carriage to drive home. He was in
the habit of shrinking back in his seat so as not to be seen by
passersby in the often crowded streets. He huddled up in the
corner again today. But after he'd gone some way he felt
curiously drawn toward the carriage door. Something beyond
the window was calling him insistently. Eventually he broke
with his custom and craned forward, and through the mist
made by his breath on the glass he saw he was driving past the
central park. The almond trees are in bloom, he thought. He
was moved. And though he almost shrank back in his corner
again, as he usually did at once after something outside had
attracted his attention, he now found himself unable to do so.
There, a few paces away, was life reviving, warmer clouds,

storks, love—all the things he'd been pretending to ignore for fear of being wrested from the grasp of the Palace of Dreams. He felt that if he was crouching there it was to protect himself, and that if ever, some late afternoon like this, he gave in to the call of life and left his refuge, the spell would be broken. The wind would turn against the Quprilis and the men would come for him as they'd come for Kurt, and take him, perhaps a little less unceremoniously, to the place from which there is no returning.

But despite these thoughts he didn't take his face away from the window. I'll order the sculptor right away to carve a branch of flowering almond on my tombstone, he thought. He wiped the mist off the window with his hand, but what he saw outside was still no clearer; everything was distorted and iridescent. Then he realized his eyes were full of tears.

T i r a n a
1981

Born in 1936 in the Albanian mountain town of Girokaster, near the Greek border, Ismail Kadare studied in Tirana and at the Gorki Institute, Moscow. He is Albania's greatest living poet and novelist, whose works have been translated worldwide. He established an uneasy *modus vivendi* with the Communist authorities until their attempts to turn his reputation to their advantage drove him in October 1990 to seek asylum in France, for, as he says, "Dictatorship and authentic literature are incompatible. . . . The writer is the natural enemy of dictatorship."

 The Palace of Dreams, which appeared in Albania in 1981 and was immediately banned, arose out of Kadare's long-nurtured ambition to invent a hell of his own. "I kept weighing up what an ambitious and over-fanciful proposal this was, though," he wrote, "after those unknown Egyptians, after Virgil, Saint Augustine and, above all, Dante. . . ."